FOREST SHADOW

David W. Cropper

Cat Man Publushing

Copyright © 2023 by David W. Cropper

All rights reserved. No part of this publication may be reproduced, stored, or transmitted in any form or by any means, electronic, mechanical, photocopying, recording, scanning, or otherwise, without written permission from the publisher. It is illegal to copy this book, post it to a website, or distribute it by any other means without written permission from the publisher or author as permitted by U.S. copyright. catmanpublishing@gmail.com.

This novel is entirely a work of fiction. The names, characters, and incidents portrayed in it are a work of the author's imagination. Any resemblance to actual persons, alive or dead, events or localities is entirely coincidental.

Cover Illustration: Joelle Cathleen

Second Edition published by Cat Man Publishing LLC. 2024

979-8-9890530-1-8 Hardback

979-8-9890530-0-1 Paperback

Library of Congress Control Number 2024913595

CONTENTS

1. Back to the forest — 1
2. The Sheriff — 13
3. What's in a dream — 23
4. The Occult store — 34
5. Jax & the Ghost — 44
6. Death is the Beginning — 54
7. Destiny — 64
8. Who to trust? — 73
9. Girl under the bridge — 83
10. Suspect arrested — 92
11. Another mess — 100
12. Everyone connected? — 109
13. Jax's story — 117
14. Call of the Shadow — 125
15. Analee's tale — 133
16. Search for memory — 141

17. Call the Spirit 150
18. Memory restored 158
19. The Circle 167
20. Forest cats 176

Chapter 1

BACK TO THE FOREST

The forest is a place of mystery and fear, where darkness seeps from every shadowy corner. Those who dare venture inside risk losing not only their way but also their very souls.

For what felt like hours, Crox wandered through the dense forest. It was located off a secluded road in Stafford County, Virginia, near where his cousin Danny had lived before he died on this very road. Crox was a middle-aged real estate broker with short red hair and piercing green eyes.

He stood at an average height of 5'9" and weighed proportionally. His left-handedness and dry sense of humor were the only unusual things about him. Crox was also passionate about music and would dance to any fast-paced tune.

Crox grew up in poverty in Fredericksburg, Virginia, just ten miles south of his current location. He spent his childhood days in a rundown single-wide trailer with his mother and three brothers. His early years were difficult, but he struggled to recall any specific memories from that time.

Instead, there were significant gaps in his recollection of the past. Despite his challenging upbringing, Crox had become a successful business owner and well-respected community leader, eagerly anticipating retirement. So why was he now wandering through a dense forest at midnight? What had drawn him to this dark and secluded place?

As Crox drove from his home in downtown Fredericksburg to this isolated spot in the late hours of the night, he didn't encounter a single car or person on the road. It was odd for a small city like this to be so deserted, even in the late hours. He couldn't quite explain why he felt compelled to come here, deep into the woods off an old country road.

But something was pulling him toward it, something he couldn't resist. Now, in the dark forest, the further he went, the more uneasy he became. Memories of a past accident flooded back to him; the last time he was here, many years ago, he had flipped his car near the same spot where he had just parked. Miraculously, he survived thanks to a mysterious cat with striking green eyes that appeared out of nowhere.

In his youth, Crox had been reckless and daring while driving his beat-up old 1978 Pontiac Grand Prix. He pushed the limits of speed, but things took a turn for the worse when he hit a patch of loose gravel. The car spun out of control and flipped, trapping him inside.

Thankfully, a tiny kitten appeared after the crash, licking the blood from his head and keeping him conscious until help arrived.

One of the EMTs found the kitten and assumed it belonged to Crox, returning it to him in the hospital once he had recovered. To this day, Crox still doesn't know who called for help.

Crox had christened the kitten Lucky, as he truly was lucky to have survived such a terrible accident. Lucky and Crox shared a unique connection, with the kitten always knowing how to cheer up his human when he was feeling low or distressed. While most cats are known for their aloofness, Lucky was rarely seen away from Crox's side. The gray and white tabby was Crox's feline bodyguard.

Lucky was more than just a pet to Crox; he was a trusted confidant and dear friend. Their bond went beyond the typical human-animal connection, and since Lucky's passing two years ago, Crox's life had been forever altered. Before Lucky came into his life, Crox couldn't remember much of his past. He suspected that the gaps in his memory were due to brain damage from an accident.

The memories of Lucky, though, were still vivid and bittersweet, always bringing a smile to his face but also tears to his eyes. Lucky had given him a new lease on life, and Crox was eternally grateful for that. If it weren't for Lucky, things may have turned out differently during the accident. He knew how lucky he was to be alive, all thanks to this special cat who had entered his world.

Crox felt an overwhelming sense of emptiness as he aimlessly wandered through the forest, plagued by the same fear and dread that had consumed him after the car accident. Lucky was no longer here to protect him. He didn't know what drew him back to this place or what he hoped to discover. Lost and without any clear direction.

Crox followed a path through the dense trees and underbrush, hoping it would lead him somewhere that would tell him why he was here at this god-forsaken hour.

Crox found his way to a small clearing in the dense forest. Signs of human presence were spread across the ground: pieces of burnt candles and tiny glass containers. Under a large oak tree, he spotted what appeared to be an improvised altar made of tree branches placed near a circle outlined by large stones. A pentagram was etched into the soil at the center of the stone circle and scorched by fire.

The ground was disturbed, and the bushes were flattened in this area, indicating recent activity. The air felt noticeably colder here, with a strange stench hanging in the air that he couldn't quite identify. It reminded him of death, and a sinking feeling started to take over. Crox heard faint scratching against a nearby tree, but nothing was there when he looked closer in the moonlight.

He thought he heard a quiet meowing sound as he made his way through the dark woods. Frowning in confusion, he searched the area again and saw a black cat staring back at him with striking green eyes that appeared almost human under the moon's glow.

Fear crept into his mind as he tried to rationalize the situation by telling himself it was just a feral cat and posed no threat. But as the small black cat approached him without hesitation, he couldn't help but wonder about its presence in these eerie woods.

Deep within Crox's mind, he heard, "Hello there. It's about time you found me. I've been waiting." The cat was speaking to him telepathically. Crox suddenly felt a tight embrace on his body, as if someone was hugging him tightly. The feeling disappeared just as quickly as it appeared.

Crox shook his head, not wanting to believe that the cat before him was talking. In a shaky voice, he replied, "I'm not sure. I followed a trail from the road, and it led me here."

Crox let out a haunting laugh that seemed to reverberate through the forest. "Am I actually having a conversation with a damn cat? Maybe I'm going crazy," he muttered, feeling a chill run down his spine. As he reached out to pet the feline, all feelings of fear and unease disappeared, replaced by a strange sense of calm that washed over him and soothed his nerves.

"Did you call for me to come here tonight?" Crox asked, looking into the cat's eyes. Incredibly, he could hear the response in his mind: Yes, there are spirits all around us. We are not alone in this forest. They need your help.

"What do they want?" Crox asked. The cat replied, "To be set free. To find peace." The words came directly into Crox's mind, sending shivers down his spine and almost causing him to faint. This was far from normal, and he began to question his sanity. Crox picked up the black cat and made his way back toward the road. He couldn't shake off the feeling that something or someone was following him, but he dared not look back for fear of what he might see.

The forest grew darker, and the moons and stars faded, leaving only their dim light to guide his way. Fear consumed him as he pushed forward, sweat pouring down his face. He broke into a run until he tripped over a tree root and crashed onto the ground. At that moment, the black cat scurried up to him and encouraged him to get back up, sensing danger lurking in the darkness. Though his vision was limited, he could feel a presence in the forest, getting closer with each passing moment.

Suddenly, something rustled in the shadows next to him. Startled, Crox scrambled to his feet but was quickly knocked down again by a strong gust of wind. Using all fours, he managed to stand up and sprint through the trees towards the road before whatever was chasing him could catch up.

With the cat safely tucked in his arms, he approached the road. Once he reached his truck, he hastily climbed inside and locked the doors behind him. His hand went under the seat until it found what it was searching for—his Smith & Wesson .38 pistol. The familiar weight of the gun made him feel safe.

Sitting there, still trying to process what had just happened, Crox held the gun tight in his hands. It all felt like a strange dream. Why did he feel such a strong pull to return to this forest? Was he starting to understand this mysterious cat telepathically? The black feline placed its paw on his hand, and a sense of familiarity overcame him.

Crox started his Ram 4x4 and began to speed off but quickly regained control. He knew that speed and lack of focus were what led him back here in the first place, causing him to crash and nearly lose his life a few years ago in this same area. He began his journey back home through downtown Fredericksburg. Suddenly, he couldn't contain his laughter any longer, and bursts of wild giggles escaped his lips. Passersby gave him strange looks, wondering if he was losing his mind.

As he drove over the Falmouth bridge, crossing the Rappahannock River, he heard a voice in his head saying, "We have found each other again." He turned to look at the black cat sitting in the passenger seat. A chill ran down his spine as he wondered if this could be Lucky's reincarnation.

Feeling uneasy, he quickly looked away but caught sight of a young girl's face staring back at him in the rearview mirror.

Panicked, he swerved and narrowly avoided hitting the bridge's cement posts. After taking a few deep breaths to calm down, he continued home with the cat in tow, avoiding any glances in the mirror.

Once they arrived home, he brought the feline inside and pondered on what to call it. Finally, he decided on a name and addressed the cat, "Well, I guess you need a name now."

A quick response came back to him: *I have a name, and it is Jax.*

"Well, nice to meet you, Jax," Crox responded, and then, under his breath, he said, " What the hell is going on..."

Back at his home, Crox made the two of them dinner, sharing a can of tuna fish with crackers while he drank a large glass of bourbon and then another. He wanted to get drunk and put this night behind him. As the night wore on, the alcohol finally took its toll on him, causing him to pass out on the couch. But his sleep was far from peaceful. In his intoxicated slumber, Crox found himself dreaming of a young girl with long auburn hair darting through a dark forest. She was dressed in tattered clothes and had a bruise forming over her left eye. Her cries for help echoed through his mind as tears streaked down her dirt-stained face. The girl seemed strangely familiar to Crox, and he kept hearing her desperate plea: "Please find my mom; she can help us."

The next morning, Crox woke up feeling disoriented and hungover, with a throbbing headache at the forefront of his brain. As he stumbled into the bathroom, he was shocked by his reflection in the mirror. His once vibrant red hair was now completely gray, and his skin had taken on a translucent quality. More freckles sprinkled across his nose, and his eyes had a hardened look as if he had lived a life filled with regret and wrongdoing. There also was the beginning of a bruise just under his left eye.

The figure in the mirror was unrecognizable; his eyes were filled with a crazed and desperate look. In a fit of panic and fear, he punched through the glass, letting out a deafening scream as shards fell around him. Was he losing his mind? What was happening to him? Crox wondered if the black cat he had encountered earlier had brought some curse upon him. He turned to see Jax, the cat, calmly observing him from the corner. "What have I gotten myself into?" he thought, hoping it was all just a dream. But then, he heard a voice in his head telling him that this was no mere dream. It claimed there were spirits in the forest who knew him and that he had a purpose to fulfill. The voice offered its service to guide him towards his destiny.

He was struggling and needed someone to confide in, but he didn't know who to turn to. Who among his friends would understand something so bizarre? He didn't want to end up in a mental institution, with doctors in white lab coats tying him up. One person came to mind: Vonda, or as she liked to call herself, "The Vonderful Vonda." She was just the right amount of crazy to believe him. They had been good friends for years, ever since they met at a nightclub in Washington D.C. when she approached him and asked, "Who are you, cutie? I'm the Vonderful Vonda, let's dance."

Vonda was a free spirit who didn't believe in conforming to society's expectations, yet she had achieved great success. Her long, platinum-blonde hair, piercing blue eyes, and dazzling smile made her stand out wherever she went. But it wasn't just her looks that set her apart - she was also incredibly intelligent. In any challenging situation, Vonda's positivity shone through; it was infectious and could lift anyone's spirits, especially Crox, during his darkest moments. Crox called his friend for comfort, and Vonda suggested they get together and bring his new cat.

Crox arrived at Vonda's home, Honey Suckle Hill. It was a beautiful three-acre estate situated high up a hill, accessible only by a secluded country road. As he pulled up the long driveway, Crox couldn't help but admire the large oak trees on either side of him. The house had an unusual horseshoe shape with a courtyard in the middle and a pool and hot tub in the back. Clearly, this home was meant for entertaining, and Vonda was known for throwing extravagant adult-only parties.

Crox purposely omitted all the details when he told Vonda he found a cat. He felt that it was something they needed to discuss in person, over a bottle of wine or maybe two. Crox parked next to Vonda's baby blue Jaguar and sat there for a moment, and he couldn't help but laugh at the stark contrast between his large 4 x 4 truck and her small sports car. They had both come a long way since they met.

He couldn't help but feel proud of what the two of them had accomplished over the last couple of decades. It's incredible how much your life can transform over just a few short years. He and Vonda both overcame the challenges of growing up in poverty with determination and a little luck. Some asshole once told him, "For a boy from the trailer park, you've done quite well." It was meant as a subtle insult, but he brushed it off because he knew it was true. He had achieved great success and could be proud of his accomplishments.

Looking down at Jax, there on Vonda's doorstep, less than 24 hours since his return to the forest, Crox realized that his life would never be the same again. Jax purred contentedly, almost as if in agreement with him. Vonda greeted him with a glass of chardonnay and a warm embrace. She wasted no time telling him to change and join her in the hot tub, a routine they had established together. For this very reason, he always had spare clothes at her place.

Vonda and Crox settled into the hot tub, leaving Jax to explore the backyard on his own. He leaned back and let the warm water envelop him, sipping his wine and feeling the stress slowly melt away. Suddenly, Vonda gave him a severe look and asked, "What's going on with you? You look terrible." Crox let out a heavy sigh, knowing this conversation was inevitable. He told her about everything that had happened in the past day.

When Crox was done with his tale, Vonda sat quietly for a moment and then said, "Why on earth did you go back to that place where you almost died? Ramouth Church Road and the surrounding forest are not places for you. I know that road is a dark place, and there are tales of witches having occult ceremonies in those woods, Crox, now make me a promise: you won't go back there."

Crox reminded Vonda he had grown up near Ramouth Church Road and knew the stories of the disappearances and murders that had occurred over the years. "Last night, something called me there; I can't explain it, and finding another cat can't be a coincidence. And this cat speaks to me telepathically." Crox continued, "You have to believe me; I'm not making this up."

Crox also told Vonda about seeing the girl in his rearview mirror and his dream of the same girl. Vonda looked back at him and said, "Well, either you are going insane or smoking something. Cats don't talk. Just then, Jax jumped onto the edge of the hot tub, knocking Vonda's glass of wine over.

Crox could feel that strange energy through his body as he heard it in his mind. Jax told him a leak from Vonda's pool was draining into the septic system, causing it to overflow into the backyard's far east end. Crox informed Vonda of what the cat had told him.

"How the hell would you know that?" Vonda asked snippily. Crox shrugged. "Jax just told me." Vonda stood up, got out of the hot tub, and looked at the back of the property. Sure enough, water and sewage were seeping up from the ground at the back eastern side of the property.

Vonda's scream of anger pierced the air, causing chills to run up Crox's spine. Her voice held a hint of fear, which only intensified his apprehension. Vonda quickly shut off the water valve for the pool and returned to sit in the hot tub, pouring herself another glass of wine. After taking a big gulp, she asked Crox to recount everything that had happened, leaving no details out. As he told her the entire story, he couldn't shake the feeling that something had always been off about Ramouth Church Road. Vonda looked into his eyes and saw a fear in him she had never seen before. At that moment, she also began to feel afraid - both for Crox and of him.

Jax looked at Vonda with an air of superiority as if to say, *I told you so.*

"Ok, I believe you, so now what? Vonda asked.

I want to know if this little girl in my dream is real and what may have happened to her." Crox responded.

"I think I may know someone who can help you." Vonda stated, "Relda Michealson is familiar with Stafford County and the goings-on at Ramouth Church Road; she's from the area, her family has been here for more than six generations, and her great-great-grandfather was one of the enslaved people who built the old Ramouth Church. I am sure she or someone in her family will know the folklore and shine some light on the area."

Crox was familiar with Relda; she had been a regular at Honey Suckle Hill on and off over the years.

Despite being a law enforcement officer, she also enjoyed having a good time. Recently, Relda had been promoted to Sheriff. Would she believe his story about a cat who spoke to him telepathically, could see ghosts, and wanted to save them?

Crox had no idea what the ghost needed saving from, but he knew he needed help. Vonda contacted Relda and arranged to meet with her later in the week. She didn't mention the details of the talking cat, not wanting to be dismissed as crazy by Relda.

Chapter 2

The Sheriff

Crox was familiar with Relda; she had been a Honey Suckle Hill regular over the years. Despite being a law enforcement officer, she also enjoyed having a good time. Recently, Relda had been promoted to Sheriff. Would she believe his story about a cat who spoke to him telepathically, could see ghosts, and wanted to save them?

Crox had no idea what the ghost needed saving from, but he knew he needed help. Vonda contacted Relda and arranged to meet with her later in the week. She didn't mention the details of the talking cat, not wanting to be dismissed as crazy by Relda.

Driving away from Honey Suckle Hill with Jax curled up next to him in the front seat, Crox headed home, feeling better that he had opened up to Vonda. After arriving at his house, Crox cooked them a tuna fish and crackers meal.

While they ate, he reflected on his day with Vonda. Despite feeling a bit foolish, he couldn't help but feel optimistic. Was he reading too much into things? Jax sat in the corner, gazing up at him from his food dish with soulful eyes and a smile on his feline face. Crox hoped for a good night's rest; his body was sore and exhausted from his stress, and the hot tub's effects had quickly worn off.

The dreams came quickly, engulfing him in a thicket of towering trees whose branches intertwined like fingers grasping for the sky. The air was thick with the scent of pine and damp earth, and the ground was soft beneath his feet. In the distance, a young girl darted through the trees, her wild hair flying behind her as she ran. She seemed to be fleeing from some unseen danger, her cries for help echoing through the forest.

Glimpses of the pursuer—a dark, shadowy shape that seemed to shift and contort, never fully revealing itself. It remained elusive. The young girl was terrified as she tried to get away. No matter how fast she ran, the Shadowy figure was always at arm's length. Long shadowy figures reached out to grab the girl by her arm.

He awoke suddenly, a cold sweat covering his whole body. Jax jumped on his chest. In his mind, he heard Jax say; *The girl is reliving her death. She is here with us.*

Crox sprang out of bed and frantically scanned the room, but no one was there. He was alone with Jax. Yet, he couldn't shake off the feeling of a presence. The smell of dampness and rot lingered in the air, surrounding him in the room.

The following days dragged on, each one passing by agonizingly slow. The same dreams would haunt him every night, leaving him feeling drained and exhausted in the morning.

Crox desperately wanted to talk to Relda; he just had a gut feeling that his mysterious dreams and his newfound feline friend were somehow connected. But how?

The morning of his meeting with Relda, Crox went to the library and searched old newspapers in the basement. He was looking for information about cults, the history of Rammouth Church Road and the surrounding forest, and reports about missing persons. His phone rang as he dug through the stacks of old newspapers. It was Vonda, telling him Relda was ready to meet him. It was time to see the Sheriff! He grabbed his stuff and hurried out the door.

Relda was already waiting for him when he reached the Sheriff's office on Courthouse Road in Stafford County. She gave him a skeptical look and spoke to him as if he were a child. He couldn't blame her; his story probably sounded like pure madness. Vonda had briefed Relda on the situation with Jax and his recurring nightmares.

Crox took a deep breath and began recounting everything, starting from the car accident to finding Jax and his extraordinary abilities, using his own words. Relda's expression changed from surprise to a mixture of annoyance and amusement as he spoke.

Relda's presence demanded attention whenever she walked into a room. Her stunning dark complexion, accentuated by her voluptuous figure, exuded self-assuredness and poise. Her long, shapely legs could turn the head of any man, regardless of his sexual orientation.

But it was not just her natural beauty that drew people in; her warm nature and genuine kindness kept them coming back to her. Relda carried herself with confidence and grace, always wearing a radiant smile and exuding magnetic charm that made her approachable and easy to talk to.

Beneath Relda's captivating exterior lay a driven and ambitious individual. She excelled in her career and became one of the youngest sheriffs in Stafford County.

Relda and Vonda had attempted to pursue a romantic relationship, but it didn't work out. They realized they were better suited as friends. Despite their breakup, they still maintained a strong emotional connection. When Vonda came to Relda with his bizarre story, she felt obligated to listen.

As he spoke about his dreams and Jax communicating with him telepathically, Relda struggled to comprehend it all. But she could see the pain and anguish in Vonda's expression, which made her want to understand more.

Relda hesitantly agreed to assist him in searching for any recent disappearances or deaths in the vicinity through old case files. She also decided to join him on his return trip to the forest, where he found Jax and look around. They arranged to meet the next day at the abandoned Ramouth Church. While digging through cold case files after Crox left the Sheriff's office, Relda came across a report of a young girl who went missing in these woods a year ago that matched the description Crox had given her.

The next day, Crox met Relda at Ramouth Church; he had parked next to the cemetery, where many of his own family were laid to rest. The two of them headed together to where he had his accident and found Lucky and Jax. As they walked around, he could not find the spot where he had seen the circle of rocks and the pentagram that was burned into the ground.

Tired of walking in circles, Relda said she had to return to her office. Crox thanked her for her time and suggested they try again. Relda agreed with a sigh, not even trying to hide her annoyance at a wasted morning.

Crox returned home and spent the rest of the day doing household chores and sitting on the back deck reading an old Stephen King book he had read multiple times. Around midnight, Crox found himself curled up in bed with Jax beside him, Jax's eyes glimmering in the moonlight. He thought of his cousin Danny, who had lived on Ramouth Church Road and had died many years ago on that very road. The funny thing was he had not thought of Danny in a long time and now wished he was around to talk to.

Once again, the dreams invaded his sleep that night. The setting was all too familiar - a peaceful meadow with a magnificent oak tree providing shade from the sun. His cousin Danny stood beneath the tree, his golden hair blowing in the wind as he smirked at him. Danny's words sliced through the silence as he approached, "What kind of trouble have you gotten yourself into now?" Speechless, Crox could only stand there and wonder how his cousin knew about his wanderings in the forest. He woke up to Jax licking his face and purring contently. He felt an overwhelming sense of fear but couldn't pinpoint why. Shivering, he closed his eyes and hoped for some rest while relying on Jax's presence to keep him anchored to reality.

As the sun rose, Crox went through his morning routine. He hurriedly dressed, grabbed his keys, and left the house, with Jax trotting close behind him. Despite the cheerful weather and clear blue sky, a sense of hopelessness lingered within him. He climbed into his truck, took a deep breath, and drove to meet Relda at Mason Dixon Café. It was a local spot not too far from his home in downtown Fredericksburg. As soon as he arrived, he saw Relda sitting inside. She had already ordered coffee for both of them and added a dash of brandy for an extra kick. "I thought you could use something stronger this morning," she said with a knowing smile.

Thumping a large file folder onto the table, Relda began, "This is the case of Starleena Diamond, a young girl who disappeared last year. She fits the description of the girl in your dream: eleven years old with long red hair and green eyes." Relda added, "Her father, Jaxson Diamond, was also involved in the search for her but, unfortunately, was found dead on Ramouth Church Road a couple of days after she went missing from a fall where he hit his head on a rock."

Crox was taken aback when he heard the name Jaxson. Relda quickly interjected, "It's strange that you named the cat after a man who died near where you found it."

Confused, Crox replied, "I didn't give him his name; he told me what it was."

Relda's file had a news article from the previous year about Starleena going missing from her family's property on Ramouth Church Road, off Kellogg's Mill Road. She never returned. A search party by the local police and many concerned citizens turned up no trace of Little Starleena Diamond. After a few months, the searches were abandoned. No evidence of Starleena was ever found in the woods or in and around the property where she had lived. The case became cold and was soon shelved in a file cabinet at the Sheriff's office.

Crox's body tensed as he absorbed the information, a cold shiver running down his spine. The girl from his recurring dreams, Starleena Diamond, was missing and most likely dead. Her father, Jaxson, had died while searching for her. He couldn't understand why he felt such a strong connection to these strangers. As Relda spoke, organizing her thoughts aloud, Crox realized that they needed to take action.

"We have to keep searching," Relda stated firmly. "Tomorrow, we'll head back into the forest and conduct our own search. Get some rest."

Crox's face formed a strained smile; he was both excited and filled with dread at the thought of what they might find. His eyes fell upon Jax, who was now asleep on the table. Crox silently vowed, "We will find something out there tomorrow. I know it. "

Crox inquired about any unusual aspects of the location where Starleena vanished. Relda revealed that there were rumors and local legends surrounding the forest on Ramouth Church Road, with tales of unexplainable events. Some believed the area was cursed and claimed to have encountered bizarre figures who kidnapped anyone foolish enough to enter the woods. However, these tales were often dismissed as mere superstitions or exaggerations. Crox couldn't help but wonder if his own recurring dreams were somehow linked to Starleena's disappearance. And what about Jax? He pondered. According to the case file, there was no apparent connection between him and Starleena.

Relda suggested they visit the location where Starleena was last seen and then where Jaxson, her father, had died. He agreed he wanted to find out what happened to the little girl, not just for himself but for Starleena's family. "Is he still doing it, talking to you?" Relda said as she looked down at Jax with suspicion in her eyes. Crox only nodded his head. Jax jumped off the table and looked right at Relda before looking back at him and then meowed. "Was that a yes or a no?" Relda asked

Crox looked at Jax and then back at Relda. "I think he knows something but isn't saying anything."

The two finished their coffee brandies and then had another. Relda was on duty but did not seem to care. He noticed she, too, was looking less radiant than usual. Crox asked, "Are you feeling well? You do look a bit tired."

"I didn't get much sleep last night; I had a bad dream but can't seem to remember what happened in the dream. It woke me up at 3:20 am, and I could not get back to sleep," Relda said while yawning.

That evening, Crox slept throughout and had no dreams to haunt him. He awoke the next morning feeling more rested than he had in many days. Relda met him at 10:00 a.m. After a cup of coffee and cleaning up Jax's food dishes, they drove together in his 4x4 back to the forest to investigate what? He wasn't sure yet. Jax happily sat between the two, Purring softly.

Upon reaching Ramouth Church Road, they parked in the same spot he had before; his tire tracks were still visible. The dense forest loomed ahead, and he couldn't help but feel a shift in the atmosphere. He had always felt drawn to this area, both because of his accident and where his cousin Danny's death occurred.

But now, it seemed like something was warning him to stay away forever. Even Jax appeared on edge with fluffed fur and darting eyes. Deciding to follow Jax's lead, he let the cat out of the truck and watched as he disappeared into the thick undergrowth, beckoning them deeper into the forest.

As they followed Jax further into the dense forest, a sense of unease settled over them. The trees seemed to murmur, and eerie noises echoed through the undergrowth. Crox's heart raced with each step, but they couldn't turn back. Finally, after what felt like an eternity, they arrived at a small open space where a towering oak tree stood, reminiscent of the one from his recurring nightmare.

A mix of fear and curiosity pulsed through him. They scoured the area, and Relda's gaze fell upon an old, worn sign near the tree's base.

It read, "Beware the Shadow—Keeper of Souls." The words sent a chill down Crox's spine. Though the clearing appeared well-used, no signs of debris or human activity were found.

Relda and Crox walked in what felt like circles, constantly returning to the same spot. The sun was quickly setting, and the cold had seeped into their bones. They decided to build a fire and take a break to warm up and gather their bearings. Jax curled up next to them but did not offer any help in finding a way out of the woods. The forest took on an eerie atmosphere as the sun disappeared below the horizon. The branches of the trees twisted together like gnarled fingers, casting long, skeletal shadows across the ground. It felt like they were being watched by unseen eyes, observing their every move.

A gentle radiance glowed from the tree beside them. Crox and Relda could only stare in awe as the air surrounding the tree shimmered, almost as if it were coming to life. Suddenly, Crox felt like he had been struck by a bolt of lightning, causing him to collapse onto the ground. In his mind, he heard Jax urgently say, "Leave now!"

From the darkened shadows emerged a figure. It bore an uncanny resemblance to the shadowy apparition that had chased Starleena in his dreams. With a commanding tone, Relda yelled, "Get away from us, Devil." The shadowy figure vanished, seemingly taken aback by Relda's boldness.

Relda looked at him, fear in her eyes, but her voice was steady when she said. "I don't know what the hell that was, and I am not staying here to find out. Grab that damn cat, and let's get the hell out of here."

The path seemed to widen as they raced back to his truck. This time, they did not get lost. As they returned to the vehicle, he heard in his mind, *Fear the Shadow*.

Crox looked down at Jax as he telepathically transmitted one final thought: *Starleena had been lost to the Shadow. Help her and bring this darkness to an end.*

As he drove home, his mind struggled to process what had happened. Relda refused to discuss the events when he arrived and promised to call him tomorrow. She quickly got into her car and drove away.

As he prepared for bed, Crox hoped for a peaceful night without disturbing dreams. Unfortunately, this wish would not be granted. He would experience one of his life's most intense and terrifying dreams.

It was clear that he needed to start seeing his dreams as a way to communicate with the other side if he wanted to survive what lay ahead. Little did he know the evil and danger that awaited him. However, Jax was fully aware of the threat they were both about to face.

Chapter 3

What's in a Dream

Crox's sleep was restless; he tossed and turned, letting out soft moans. Jax sat nearby, watching over his companion with a protective gaze. The cat seemed to sense the impending doom of this dream but could do nothing to prevent it. In his unconscious state, he found himself descending deeper into the woods; the trees grew thicker, and a chill permeated the air. He exhaled, watching his breath form clouds in front of him. Every rustle of leaves echoed in the stillness of the night, amplifying his fear.

The moon cast eerie shadows on the forest floor. An unsettling feeling washed over him like a lover's embrace, except it was unwelcome and suffocating. He couldn't shake off the feeling that unseen eyes were watching his every move.

Suddenly, a dark figure darted between the trees coming toward him. Panic seized him tightly. Crox turned and ran, hoping to escape whatever was chasing him as he delved deeper into the dense forest. With each step, his fear grew as he realized he had no idea where he was or how to escape this prison of trees.

The shadowy figure drew nearer, a shapeless darkness that moved with an eerie grace between the trees. It felt like a phantom or a demon from hell. This was not a being of flesh and blood. The Shadow hovered slightly above the ground, never touching it. Its piercing shriek filled the air.

Each time Crox dared to glance back, the figure had closed the distance, its features still indistinguishable, heightening his fear. He sprinted through the dense underbrush, frantically searching for a way out. But the forest seemed to conspire against him - branches snatching at his clothes, roots tripping his steps, and darkness closing in. Even the light from the moon and stars offered no light to see by, leaving him lost in the darkness of the woods.

Despite the mounting fear, his will to survive pushed him forward. He refused to let death claim him on this night. The forest seemed to morph and warp around him as he darted through the towering trees. Spindly branches reached out like clawed hands, threatening to ensnare him. The chase felt like it would never end, dragging on endlessly. Exhausted and terrified, he stumbled upon a stone structure tucked away in the forest's depths. The arch over the doorway was adorned with handwritten words in a foreign language that he could not decipher.

Crox hesitated at the entrance, fearing what lay inside. But he had to find a hiding place, so he hoped the Shadowy figure wouldn't follow him. The structure's interior was even colder than the forest outside and devoid of any light.

Nevertheless, he prayed it would provide a brief respite from the relentless pursuit and give him time to recover his energy. He rummaged through his pockets and found a book of matches, which he used to light one after another, trying to steady his pounding heart with deep breaths. He scanned the dimly lit space anxiously but couldn't spot anyone - especially not the shadow figure. Despite the bone-chilling dampness, he felt a sense of security within these sturdy stone walls.

Looking around, Crox saw no place he could hide. The building had only one large room, with what appeared to be an altar in the middle. He slowly approached the stone shrine, where he saw a hand mirror with a knife lying on top of it. The knife had a long blade with a pearl handle. There was writing on the blade, but he could not make out what it said, just like the writing over the doorframe; this writing was also of a language he did not know. The hand mirror was made of silver, with carvings of cats on the back of it.

Crox picked up the knife and looked into the mirror. He did not see his reflection but instead saw Starleena staring back at him with tears in her eyes. All of a sudden, she let out a horrific scream, causing him to drop the mirror on the ground, shattering it into tiny pieces. The minutes passed in maddening silence. It became evident that the shadowy figure had not followed him into this ancient structure. He was thankful but knew he could not stay there for long, as the Shadow could appear at any moment. He decided to leave his safe place and go back into the forest. Crox slowly walked out of the doorway. He saw that the moon was now high in the sky, and the stars twinkled brightly. It gave him much-needed light to see to escape from this hellish place.

Crox couldn't shake off the feeling of being watched. Finally, as the first rays of sunlight broke through the dense foliage, he stumbled upon a deserted road, gripping his knife tightly. He was grateful to be out of the eerie woods, but just as he stepped onto the road, a hand grabbed his shoulder and spun him around. It was Danny, his cousin, who looked worse for wear with torn clothes, blood dripping down his face, and dirt matted in his blonde hair. He shook Crox vigorously and shouted, "Beware the Shadow-Keeper of Souls!" Without thinking, Crox stabbed Danny's left eye with his knife.

Crox jolted awake, still hearing the pained howls of pain from his cousin ringing in his ears. Panicked, he tumbled out of bed and knocked over the nightstand, causing him to fall on the floor and knock his head on the corner of the bedpost. Jax quickly ran to his side, meowing and licking his forehead where he had hit it. The sensation was eerily familiar- it reminded him of his old cat Lucky, who had licked the same spot after the car accident that left him trapped and bleeding. Crox couldn't shake off the feeling that this dream held some warning, but his thoughts were interrupted by Jax's claws digging into his stomach as the cat kneaded him. Then, he heard Jax speak in his mind: "You must find the Shadow to break this curse and save Starleena. It is your destiny."

Crox stumbled to his feet and headed to the kitchen, unable to shake the lingering fear from his dream. The nightmare had spooked him, and he felt like he was being watched by something just outside his window. He made a cup of coffee and settled at the kitchen table. Relda had sent him a text earlier, asking him to call her. He dialed her number, and Relda picked up the phone after a few rings. " Good Morning; What's shaking, Boo?"

"Morning Relda, something happened last night, something strange. I had a dream about this shadowy figure chasing me through the forest, and then I saw Starleena in a mirror. When I tried to escape, my dead cousin Danny appeared and told me, 'Beware the Shadow-Keeper of souls,' and then I stabbed him in the eye."

Relda listened in silence. All he heard was her heavy breathing. Finally, she said, "Didn't Danny die years ago? That was long before Starleena went missing. Why do you think this dream is connected to Starleena's disappearance? Do you think he could have known her or her family?" Relda asked.

"I'm not sure if they were connected," Crox replied. "But it's strange that I dreamt of him along with the Shadow figure. He didn't know Starleena or her family, as far as I know. But he did live close by." Crox had dreams about Danny since his death, but this was the first time he saw him so clearly. In previous dreams, they would meet in a meadow under a large oak tree and talk, but Crox could never recall their conversations upon waking.

Crox spoke slowly, saying, "I believe Danny is attempting to convey something from the spirit realm. He may know what happened to Starleena and is possibly trying to aid me or stop me from delving deeper into it. I'm not sure which." Relda sighed and replied, "Okay, let's go check out that commune where Starleena resided. Maybe we can gather more information there. I'll handle the talking. Be prepared to leave as soon as I arrive."

Relda arrived in her police cruiser to pick him up an hour later. She suggested she drive her squad car, as people living on the property owned by Jaxson Diamond called the commune might be more willing to talk to them if she was in uniform and showed up in a police vehicle.

Crox wasn't sure they should show up in a police car but knew he had no choice, so he kept his mouth shut. They drove off with Jax curled up in the back seat; he looked like a kitty felon on his way to the pokey.

The entrance to the commune was on Kellogg Mill Road at the commune, off Ramouth Church Road. A twenty-acre property that Jaxson Diamond purchased Fifteen years ago, although there was no record of him having a job. Crox had looked up the property's public record through his real estate systems. He was also able to verify the property was bought in cash. The property consisted of one old house and four broken-down single-wide trailers. He assumed perhaps twelve people were living on the land.

As they approached the property, a locked chain connected to a steel post blocked their way. Relda pulled the car over and honked the horn, causing a middle-aged woman to emerge from a shed-like structure and approach the police car. The woman's tone was short and cold as she asked what they wanted, reminding them that this was private property. Relda quickly flashed her badge and explained that they were there to investigate the disappearance of Starleena Diamond. The woman's frown deepened, but she begrudgingly removed the chain to allow them to enter the commune.

They drove up the lengthy driveway and parked in front of a dilapidated house in dire need of fresh paint. The porch sagged under their weight, and some windows were boarded up. The place exuded a sense of sorrow and despair. Three men and two women stood on the porch, observing a group of kids playing kickball in the open field nearby. The adults eyed the newcomers suspiciously, but the children did not heed them. Relda displayed her badge and began questioning the group about Starleena's disappearance.

They only learned that Analee Morgan, Starleena's mother, had left the commune. The men were more talkative than the women, who seemed afraid and unwilling to speak. After persistent questioning, they finally found one person willing to engage in conversation.

She was a young girl who had been playing kickball. She left her game and approached Relda, listening intently as she asked her questions. The young girl revealed that she was a friend of Starleena's. Her name was Reba, and she was perhaps twelve years old. Her hair was a rich, deep shade of brown, cascading waves just below her shoulders, framing her face with a touch of untamed charm. She seemed to trust them.

"I believe the thing living in the forest took Starleena. She didn't leave home." Reba continued."That creature also caused Starleena's dad's death. He didn't die from a simple fall. His body was mangled."She went on to explain she had been with the searchers who found his body in the woods.

Crox listened in silence as if he was frozen in place. Finally, he found his voice, and he said slowly to Relda. "Should we drop this now? I don't want to end up dead in the woods." Relda looked at him and said, "Don't be silly. I will protect you."

Relda looked back at the girl. "Do you know where we can find Analee, Starleena's mother?" Reba shook her head. "No, but I know someone who might know."

Reba walked them over to a nearby trailer. There, they met an old white-haired man with a walking stick; at the top of it was a carved head of a cobra with ruby gems for its eyes. He introduced himself as Jacob. He welcomed them to come in and have a seat. The furniture was mismatched and old but oddly comfortable. He offered them a glass of homemade moonshine.

Relda was on duty and reluctant to accept the alcohol, but at Jacob's urging, she gave in and drank the offering.

Jacob advised that he had known Analee since she and Jaxson got together. They had invited him to live here at the commune about three years ago. He then told them Analee had just up and left one day soon after Jaxson was found dead. Analee had just up and left without telling anyone she was leaving. He had not seen her since the day she left the commune.

According to Jacob, Analee used to work at a small occult bookstore called "Galinda, the Good Witch: Books, Curiosities, and Notions" on Caroline Street in downtown Fredericksburg. The shop was popular among those who identified as witches and practiced various forms of the Wiccan religion. Analee shared an interest in witchcraft and may have sought out guidance from the owner or employees there. Relda thanked Jacob for his insight and suggested they move on, as she didn't believe any other residents would have useful information to offer.

On their drive back to Fredericksburg, Crox and Relda discussed what they knew so far, which wasn't much. Analee may be involved with witchcraft and works at an occult shop. Did she have a role in Starleena's disappearance or her husband's death? Was the shadowy figure from his nightmare connected?

They went to downtown Fredericksburg to visit "Galinda the Good Witch: Books, Curiosities, and Notions." A "closed" sign was hanging in the door window when they arrived. They would have to come back another day when the shop was open. Crox heard in his mind Jax say, *There are answers here. But be cautious.*

Crox's uneasiness grew as he looked at Relda, but she seemed unfazed by whatever had come over him.

Crox decided to keep his strange feelings to himself for now. However, he realized he had forgotten his coat in Jacob's trailer and asked Relda to return to the commune to retrieve it. Instead of going straight to Jacob's front door, Crox felt drawn to the side of the trailer for some reason.

He spotted his coat hanging on a tire swing tied to a large tree as he walked around. He grabbed it and headed back to the car, but something caught his eye. Half buried under a yellow rose bush was a large knife with a blade that glistened like pure silver and a handle that resembled a fine white pearl. The moon and stars above reflected off the blade as Crox carefully picked it up and tucked it into his coat pocket. He couldn't shake off the feeling that this knife would come in handy soon enough.

The two of them drove away in silence. He did not tell Relda about the knife because he had basically stolen it, and Relda was, after all, a cop. During the car ride, he heard Jax purr as if he agreed to keep quiet. He and Relda would return to the shop Galinda the Good Witch: Books, Curiosities, and Notions another time. Hopefully, they would learn more about Analee Morgan, why she left the area, and where she lived.

As they approached his home, he felt his anticipation and excitement growing. Jax jumped in the front seat next to him and pawed at his side. He felt the knife in his pocket. He wondered if this knife would help him find the answers he was searching for or if he had just stolen an old man's possession for no reason. Time would tell, he assumed. Relda bid him and Jax ado and drove off, leaving them to their own devices. After a heavy dinner and a bad movie on Netflix, Jax went to his favorite chair and drifted off to a sound and deep sleep.

Crox, on the other hand, found himself in yet another dream, wandering deep into a forest. He was again searching for the lost girl, Starleena, who had disappeared without a trace. Despite the townsfolk warning him of the forest's deadly reputation, in his dream, he was determined to find the young girl and bring her back to her family. A soft rustling sound caught his attention as he ventured deeper into the dark woods. He turned a beautiful black cat with striking green eyes that seemed to glow like stars. It was Jax. The cat looked at him and spoke out loud. "I am the guardian of these woods." The cat's voice was surprisingly calm and soothing. It also had a familiar sound, but Crox could not place it.

He was astonished to find himself conversing with Jax out loud and not within his mind. "I seek to find a lost girl named Starleena Diamond. Can you help me find her?" He asked. Jax fixed his gaze on him and replied, "I know of the girl you seek, but you must understand the danger ahead. If you continue on this path, you are sure to meet your death." Though skeptical of the cat's warning, Crox felt an inexplicable truth in the cat's words. "Please, I must find her and bring her back to her family," he pleaded.

Jax sighed, "Very well, I will guide you through the woods, but you must promise me to be cautious." Crox agreed, and with Jax leading the way, they ventured deeper into the heart of the forest. As they journeyed, Jax warned him of treacherous traps, hidden sinkholes, and dangerous creatures lurking in the darkness. "I appreciate your guidance, Jax," he said gratefully.

Jax replied, "I am one of the many guardians of these woods, each with a unique purpose. Some of us are tasked with taking the souls of those who stumble into our forest. Many years ago, it was my duty to take the soul of a man who had crashed his car in our woods.

However, I chose to save his life instead of fulfilling my task. But the forest still requires a soul to be taken, and it will not be denied what is owed to it."

Crox'sheart skipped a beat as he realized the cat was talking about him. Years ago, he had crashed his car in the woods, and his old cat Lucky had saved his life. Could this dream forest be that the same woods and its guardians were somehow connected to that fateful night? As they continued walking, the sound of a waterfall grew louder in the distance. Eventually, they reached the top of a hill and entered a clearing with a breathtaking waterfall pouring into a crystal-clear lake. On the other side of the lake stood a tall ivory-white marble table on a raised platform. Crox approached the table and saw a small stone with strange symbols and a warning message engraved on it. The words seemed to sear into his mind: "Beware the Shadow-Keeper of Souls."

Crox was jolted awake by the bright morning light filtering through the blinds and casting shadows across his body. As he slowly regained consciousness, he realized he was standing in front of the kitchen window, completely naked. The dream from last night still felt incredibly real to him. He looked down at his hand and saw that he was holding the knife he had stolen from the commune.

A small amount of blood stained the blade, but upon further inspection, he found no injuries on his body. Shaking his head to clear the remnants of the nightmare, he glanced over at Jax, who was perched on the countertop with a knowing expression on his feline face.

Chapter 4
The Occult Store

Crox dialed Relda's number and relayed his dream, leaving out the part about the knife. She sounded tired on the phone but agreed to meet later that day. They planned to revisit the occult shop when it was open and learn more about Analee Morgan.

While he waited for Relda to arrive, Crox decided to do some individual investigation. He opened his laptop and searched Google for information on the peculiar phrase "Beware the Shadow-Keeper of Souls" and the store known as Galinda the GoodWitch: Books, Curiosities, and Notions.

The search yielded few results. The only information he could find was that the store had been established five years earlier.

The shop was owned by Sun-Moon Peterson, with no other notable details. However, while delving into obscure occult websites, he stumbled upon an intriguing article about the phrase "Beware the Shadow-Keeper of Souls."

The vintage magazine piece that had been uploaded to a witch's chat room recounted a local legend of a cursed forest said to be plagued by a vengeful entity known as the Shadow. The story told of a tragic incident in which a family disappeared in the woods over 100 years ago, with the Shadow claiming their souls. According to the legend, the Shadow lured unsuspecting victims into the forest and trapped them there for eternity.

The more he read, the more convinced he became that the legend and his dreams were somehow connected. The knife he found must have been connected somehow; he could not shake the feeling that it held a major significance.

When Relda arrived at his house, he shared his findings with her, including the Keeper of Souls legend and the forest connection. Relda listened attentively and seemed intrigued by the information. She suggested they visit the library before going to the occult bookstore and see if they could find more historical records or old newspaper articles about the family that disappeared in the forest.

They spent hours poring over dusty books and archives at the library, searching for any mention of the cursed forest or the lost family. Finally, they came across an old newspaper article from a century before. The article told the tragic story of the family that had vanished in the forest. Their name was the Parhams—Shane and Victoria Parham, along with their young children Sierra, Page, Haley, and Dylan. According to the article, the Parham family had been on a camping trip in the local forest when they disappeared without a trace.

The forest was known for its dangerous terrain and mysterious disappearances; some locals believed the family had either drowned in a nearby lake or decided to pick up roots and leave without telling anyone. No bodies were ever recovered, and neither had any of the family camping gear turned up. They found nothing else regarding the family and headed to the occult store.

When they arrived at the bookstore, they saw it was now open for business. As they entered the shop, he felt his breath catch. Standing before them was a woman with familiar green eyes. She had high cheekbones and fair skin with freckles across her nose. She was without shoes and wore a flowing caftan dress with large bright orange flowers on. The dress was ugly, a sin, but she pulled off the outfit. He would soon find out the look that matched her personality. She welcomed them in and introduced herself as Sun-Moon.

She appeared to be around fifty years old, with multiple tattoos of symbols and writing on her arms and neck; he could not determine what they meant. She sported bright blue hair, which she wore pulled back in a tight bun, making her look like she just had a facelift. Sun-Moon gazed between them, lingering on Crox momentarily before asking what they were shopping for. Relda explained they would like to ask her some questions regarding an official matter regarding one of her employees.

He instantly felt uneasy as she spoke, and the tiny hairs on his neck raised. He took in the interior of the occult store. It was a mesmerizing space of oddities that seemed to shift and change with every step.

The store was one large room of wonders, illuminated by a chandelier of multi-colored crystals suspended from the ceiling. The walls were lined with dusty books, their spines adorned with symbols and signs that seemed to glow faintly.

The shelves were also laden with peculiar curiosities that stretched into the distance, displaying an array of magical artifacts. Potion vials in various hues lined one section, each containing elixirs promising anything from good luck to eternal youth.

In the center of the store, a massive tree sculpture stood, with silver leaves reaching toward the high ceiling. Upon closer inspection, he noticed that the leaves were not merely silver but miniature mirrors reflecting the room's interior. It felt as if the tiny mirrors were doorways to another realm. A colorful carpet adorned the floor, guiding visitors throughout the store.

Aromas of exotic incense filled the air, creating an atmosphere of calm and relaxation. An assortment of candles flickered, casting dancing shadows upon the walls, adding a sense of mystery. Sun and Moon patiently waited as they took in the scene before them.

She welcomed them to browse and gave them a brief overview of the items she sold, including spellbooks containing rituals, invocations, and chants used by magic practitioners.

Tarot cards are used for divination, providing insights into the past, present, and future. The store also carried crystal balls, which are believed to possess divinatory powers and are often used to receive visions of the dead.

She warned them to exercise caution when handling the artifacts and to read the warnings provided for each item, as some could cause serious harm.

Crox asked Sun-Moon, "Do you have an employee named Analee Morgan? We are looking to speak to her." Sun-Moon shook her head, "No, I no longer employ Analee. She used to work here but resigned about a year ago.

Relda chimed in, "Do you know where she may have gone to work? Or perhaps where she is living? "

Sun-Moon said in a brisk tone, "No, I do not. She just up and left."

Crox felt an inner knowing, a nagging suspicion that this woman knew more than she was letting on.

They thanked Sun-Moon for her time and walked out of the store. Standing on the sidewalk, Relda looked at him and said, "That *ho* is lying out her teeth."He simply said, "Damn Right."

As he turned to follow back to the police cruiser, he noticed a peculiar symbol etched over the door frame of the occult bookstore. It was the same symbol he had seen in a dream carved into the altar in the stone building from his dream. The symbol was an outline of a cat but with horns.

Relda dropped him off at home and told him she would call him in the next couple of days if she found anything else about Analee. He did not tell her about the symbol in the doorway, so he decided to try to research that himself.

When he walked into the house, Jax greeted him with his nose stuck in the air. Crox asked, "Are you pissed I left you alone?" He heard back in his mind, *Damn right, and you better not leave me alone again.*

He grabbed his laptop and went to Google, searching for any information he could find about the symbol over the doorway of the occult shop as he dug through the multiple links on ancient symbols. Jax came and sat on the couch next to him, a worried look on his feline face.

He finally came across the cat symbol etched above the entrance to the occult bookstore. The Sign of the Soul-Keeper was a powerful magical symbol believed to ward off evil spirits.

Deep in his gut, he believed this symbol and his dreams had to be connected to Starleena's disappearance. He leaned back in his chair, feeling mentally exhausted.

He was beginning to feel that his and Relda's investigation was not just to find out what happened to one girl but to find the truth about this Keeper of Souls ultimately and to stop any more innocent lives from being taken.

He had to find out why these symbols kept showing up. He finally closed his laptop and let out a deep sigh. He glanced over to the couch; Jax was still there, staring at him with a determined look. "What is it?" Crox asked. Jax replied, "You need to find the truth, but you don't have to do it alone. I will help you, even if it means risking our lives."

He was amazed. He had been so lucky to have been saved by a kitten many years ago, and now he had found another cat even more mystical. He smiled and said, "Let's get to work tomorrow."

Jax nodded, jumped from the couch, and led him to bed. As the two of them curled up beneath the covers, he said a silent prayer, hoping his dreams would be filled with answers.

The night, he brought another dream, one more familiar than the nightmares of the past few nights. He was in the open meadow. A large oak tree stood in the middle of the grassy meadow. As he approached the tree, he saw his cousin Danny smiling.

Danny's smile was warm and comforting, just like the memories he had of him from their childhood. He had always been the fun-loving and adventurous cousin...the one who would dare him to do crazy things and cheer him on when he succeeded.

Danny had tragically passed away in a car accident years ago, also on Ramouth Church Road, leaving a void in his heart that he had never fully healed.

Danny laughed, "Hey, Cuz. I have been trying to reach you, but it's not easy from where I am. I see what's been happening, and I need you to know you're on the right path. The answers are tied to your past; there is much that binds you to the forest of Ramona Church Road."

His heart swelled with a mix of joy and sadness. He wanted to hug Danny and feel his presence more tangibly, but this was a dream.

"I miss you, Danny," Crox whispered, tears welling up.

"I miss you too, but we can't dwell on the pain of my death. There's a reason you are connected to this forest and the Shadow. It's time for you to embrace your destiny."

"But how, Danny? I don't even know where to start."

"You already have the key, cousin. Trust in yourself, and trust in the connection you share with Jax. You'll find the way together," Danny said, his form fading.

Danny's image vanished before he could say anything else, and he was left alone in the meadow, the oak tree towering over him.

In the morning, he decided to look for more information about the Parhams, the family that had disappeared in the cursed forest over a century ago. He needed to understand the history of this place and how it might be linked to Shadow and Starleena's disappearance.

Throughout the day, he combed the internet, searching old records and historical documents online. There was much more information than what was available at the library. The Parhams' story was tragic, but it held crucial clues. As he pieced together fragments of information online, he started to notice patterns, symbols, and references to ancient rituals from different websites that seemed to match those in his dreams.

It seemed Shane Parham and his wife, Victoria, had both been accused of witchcraft. The whole family had been reclusively and did not intertwine with their local community. Their oldest daughter, Sierra, was once charged with robbing travelers by seducing them and then stealing their money, clothes, and horses, leaving them naked and standing on the side of the road.

The Stafford County townspeople were suspicious and scared of the family. It was said they would practice black magic in the woods.

He called Relda and shared his findings, who was equally intrigued by the connections they uncovered. Together, they decided to revisit the occult shop and confront Sun Moon to see if she knew of the happenings in the forest off Ramouth Church Road. She did own the only occult store in the area.

When they arrived at the bookstore, Sun-Moon was waiting for them with a bottle of wine at a table near the back of the shop. She looked at them with a mischievous smile. He felt he knew her, but this was only his second time meeting her.

Sun-Moon gestured for him and Relda to take a seat. The atmosphere was cool as they walked past the threshold, and he felt he was being watched.

Relda asked Sun-Moon, "Do you have any information regarding a family named Parham that went missing in the same woods as Starleena Diamond, Annalee's daughter?"

Sun-Moon's strange smile didn't waver, but her eyes seemed to shimmer with a knowing glint."The Parham family was more than what they appeared to be. They had knowledge and power beyond the understanding of ordinary folks."

Sun-Moon leaned against a bookshelf, her gaze never leaving his.

"There is a tale of a Shadow, a keeper of souls, who dwells in the woods near where that family and that little girl disappeared. Some believe it to be an entity brought to our realm through magic; its true nature is unknown. Victoria Parham was believed to be the one who brought forth the being through the practice of black magic, and her family suffered the ultimate price at the hands of this entity."

Relda crossed her arms, looking skeptical."Wait, are you saying that this Shadow thing is a real thing that this woman summoned?" Relda asked, her voice filled with doubt.

Sun-Moon nodded. "Yes, the legends are true. The witch, Victoria, was a powerful practitioner of magic, and she sought to harness the power of the Shadow for her selfish purposes.

She believed she could control it to gain power and knowledge. But the Shadow was not easily tamed and demanded a heavy price for its services.

"What happened to the Parham family then?" Crox asked, his voice tinged with apprehension.

"Legend has it that the Shadow turned against them," Sun-Moon replied. "In a fit of rage, it claimed all their souls, trapping them in the forest for eternity. Since then, the Shadow has continued to collect the souls of those who dare to enter those woods."

He felt a knot forming in his stomach."And what about the symbol, the one over your doorway shaped like a cat with horns? What does it mean to you?"

Sun-Moon's smile grew wider."The symbol acts as a calling card for those who seek the Shadow. It's also a mark of brotherhood. However, those who bear the mark may also catch the attention of the Shadow."

"But what does this have to do withAnalee or her missing daughter?" Relda asked, clearly frustrated.

Sun-Moon's gaze shifted to Relda, her eyes narrowing slightly. "Analee is a witch. She sought to uncover the secrets of the Shadow. But her curiosity led her down a dangerous path. She delved too deep into the forbidden, and her family paid the price, the same as the Parhams'."

Sun-Moon's expression turned somber. "Analee came to me seeking answers, and I tried to warn her about the dangers she was getting into. She was desperate to find a way to free the trapped souls from the Shadow's grasp."

"We need to find Analee," Crox said firmly. "Why would she just up and leave town?"

Relda chimed in, "We don't know if she is even still alive."

Sun-Moon studied him intently. "Be careful. The path you're heading on is a dangerous one.

The Shadow is not to be underestimated; a cursed forest is a place of lost souls and forgotten horrors."

Before leaving the store, Crox asked Sun-Moon one last question, "How do we protect ourselves from this Shadow creature and its evil?"

Sun-Moon leaned in and whispered, "Knowledge is your best defense against its evil. Learn of its weaknesses, as well as its origins. But be warned, the more you dive into the mysteries of the Shadow, the more likely you will be trapped by it."

Relda and Crox left the occult store, feeling like they had more questions than answers. Sun-Moon's story was more infuriating than informative.

Chapter 5

Jax & the Ghost

When Crox returned home, Jax was sitting on the kitchen counter. The place was a total disaster. The kitchen cabinets were open, and plates and glasses were broken and scattered about the floor. Little claws had shredded the living room curtains, a bag of flour was busted open, and little white paw prints were on every surface imaginable.

He stood in the doorway, taking in the chaos with wide eyes. "What in the world happened here?" Crox exclaimed, glancing at Jax, who was looking smug on the counter.

Jax's tail swished back and forth as he stared at him, feigning innocence despite the apparent mischief look in his eyes. The cat let out a soft meow, almost as if to say he was proud of his handiwork.

Inside his mind, he heard Jax say, "I had a little adventure while you were away. I had to keep myself entertained. I told you not to leave me alone again. You were warned."

As he began to clean up the mess, Jax watched with a hint of guilt in his eyes. Seeing his human upset made the cat realize he had gone too far, but then he thought, "I told him not to leave me, that there would be consequences."

After the mess was taken care of and the house put back in order, He poured himself a tall glass of bourbon, went out on his back deck, and lit a cigar, staring up at the night sky; there was a good moon which he took as a bad omen.

Jax joined him on the back porch and jumped on the chair beside him. In his mind, he heard, "Ghosts are all around us, and they are angry."

He leaned back, his eyes fixed on the bright orange amber from the end of his cigar. "What do these ghosts have to say?"

Stay away from the forest if you wish to remain alive. I know of your inquiries and will not tolerate any more nosiness. He took another puff from his cigar, mulling over Jax's words. The warning gave him pause as he took a sip of his bourbon, his mind still trying to grasp the warning.

Jax jumped down, returned to the house, lay by the front door, and slept. As he watched the cat go, he was still angry with the feline for causing such a mess in his house.

The moonlight cast long shadows across the backyard, and the rustling of leaves took on an ominous tone. It was as if the very air around him had become charged with a sense of foreboding.

Lost in his thoughts, he finished his cigar and bourbon, but unease lingered. He decided to retire for the night, hoping that a good night's sleep would clear his mind.

That night, he had a vivid dream. He was standing at the edge of a dense, dark forest, with the light from the blood moon barely penetrating through the trees. He could feel eyes watching him. Something was lurking in the woods.

A soft voice seemed to echo from all directions: "You've trespassed yet again. You were saved once; do not expect to be so again."

He awoke in a cold sweat. He grabbed his cell phone to check the time. It was 3:20 a.m.

He knew he would never get back to sleep, so he got up and made a strong pot of coffee. As the coffee brewed, he paced around the kitchen, trying to shake off the unsettling dream.

He decided that he needed to distract himself. He picked up his laptop and began watching funny Cat YouTube videos. He just wanted his mind to go blank and not think anymore of his dreams or all this craziness with Jax.

Jax came into the living room and joined him on the couch. In his mind, he heard Jax say, "Really!" as he pawed at the laptop. He chuckled and closed the computer, "I guess I should do something more productive with my time."

As he paced, he started to wish he had not stepped away full-time from his Real Estate Brokerage. Crox Home Sales Inc. had been doing well for the past decade, and a few months back, He had decided to semi-retire, leaving the day-to-day business run by his second-command Armand. The business no longer needed him for daily operations, which left him time to enjoy more leisurely activities. He was now regretting that move. If he had still been working, he would not have gotten involved with a cat who talks to him, and he definitely wouldn't be having these nightly nightmarish dreams.

As the morning sun rose, his mind was still in turmoil. He could not shake off the uneasy feelings of last night's dream. He decided to walk outside, hoping that the fresh morning air and some exercise would help calm his nerves.

As he strolled through his suburban neighborhood, he saw familiar surroundings; however, they seemed different in the early morning light. The trees appeared to cast longer shadows, and the wind carried an eerie whisper. He wondered if his strange dreams were affecting his perception of reality.

Lost in his thoughts and not paying attention, he almost bumped into his neighbor, Lola, who lived a few houses down. She was watering her plants in the front yard, wearing a tight white tank top and short denim shorts. Her dog was lying on the porch, watching his owner lazily.

Lola was an alluring woman who radiated both beauty and confidence. Her sensual allure commanded attention, turning heads as she strolled through the neighborhood with her loyal companion, Barron, a charming and spirited dog who seemed to mirror his owner's charm.

She possessed a keen intellect and a sharp wit, which she utilized to keep her finger on the pulse of the town's happenings. She was the unofficial guardian of local gossip, possessing an uncanny knack for acquiring information others might overlook.

She looked up and smiled warmly. "Good morning, neighbor!" "Good morning, Lola," he replied, trying his best to hide the anxiety that still lingered within him. He admired her ability to be so cheerful in the mornings; he never saw her in a bad mood.

Lola tilted her head slightly, noticing the hint of distress in his eyes. "Is everything alright, neighbor?" she asked with genuine concern.

"Well, it's been an eventful few days at my house. Jax, my cat, caused quite a mess in the kitchen yesterday."

He did not want to discuss more details with Lola, and he did not want her to think the people from the funny farm needed to be called in to drag him off to a padded cell.

Lola chuckled, "Oh, animals can be a handful sometimes, can't they? But they do add a lot of excitement to our lives." She gave Barron, who was now at her side wagging his tail, a pat on the head as if to emphasize her point.

He nodded, relieved that Lola did not pry any further. "Yes, they certainly do." He bid her farewell and continued his walk, returning home as the sun had fully risen. Jax was waiting patiently by the front door as he walked in.

Jax looked up at him with curious eyes, aware of the restless night he had endured. He bent down to scratch behind Jax's ears, finding comfort in petting his mischievous feline companion."All is forgiven little on."

As the day progressed, he got caught up in household chores, trying to keep his mind occupied. He cleaned, organized, and even cooked himself a hearty lunch. Yet, despite his efforts, the feeling of unease remained, with his dream replaying repeatedly in his mind.

Jax went to the backyard to bathe in the sunlight as he was busy. Starleena's ghost appeared, standing over him. Jax did not run or be disturbed by the sight of the dead girl's ghost. He listened intently as Starleena said, "Find Mom...she can save me."

Jax replied, "We are close, but he is weaker than I expected. Please give me time to prepare him."

He would have to be more persistent in getting the human to move faster and find Analee, even if it meant Crox would have to face mortal risk. Saving Starleena's soul from its prison was far more critical than this man's life.

Later that day, while Crox was busy in his home office, Jax decided to take matters into his own hands. He jumped onto the desk, knocking over unopened mail and a few papers, and then deliberately knocked over a glass of water to get his attention.

He swatted at one of the envelopes that had fallen on the floor. It contained a letter from a law firm that had not gotten around to opening. He cleaned up the water and picked up the mess. He noticed the envelope from the attorney's office and opened it. In the letter, an attorney sought to meet with him regarding an inheritance of land left to him by his brother, who had died.

As he continued to read, his heart went cold, and his mind went into a whirlwind, as he was the youngest of three boys, or so he thought. Both of his older brothers had died years ago and were penniless, and had owned nothing. As he now found out, he did have a younger brother, who died a year ago with no possible heirs, as he was not legally married. This man only had one child, who was presumed dead. The long-lost brother'sname was Jaxson Diamond.

The letter explained that his mother, nicknamed Pittapat, had remarried and had a child. So Jaxson was his half-brother.

He realized he might have had a half-brother since he had minimal contact with his family after he left home at sixteen. His mother remarrying and having another child seemed logical, he mused.

He called the lawyer's office and spoke to a secretary, who set an appointment for him later that afternoon with the attorney, Jaxson Diamond's estate executor.

As he prepared to leave for the meeting, he could not help but feel a mix of emotions. On the one hand, he was intrigued by the revelation of a long-lost brother and an inheritance of property.

On the other hand, he was not happy that his mother never told him about his brother and that he had not been able to know him; perhaps he had been a better human being than his older brothers had been.

Jax watched him prepare to leave, sensing the internal conflict within his human companion. He knew Crox needed to see the truth about their connection but also worried about the potential danger ahead. Yet, time was of the essence, and the longer they waited, the riskier it became that he would not be able to save Starleena.

As he arrived at the lawyer's office, Williams and Sharick, attorneys at law, he was greeted by an attractive middle-aged woman with short, curly brown hair and stunning violet eyes that seemed to penetrate his soul. She introduced herself as Attorney Mickie Williams. She led him into a cozy office, where they sat down to discuss the details of the inheritance.

Mickie went on to explain that Jaxson Diamond had died with limited liquid cash, although it had been enough to pay her fees and any debt that Jaxson had. He had free and clear 20 acres of land in Stafford County. It was the same secluded area he and Relda had visited. He was surprised that his long-lost brother had lived so close to him all this time.

As Mickie continued, she mentioned that Jaxson Diamond had no legal heirs except his daughter, Starleena, who had disappeared over a year ago.

If the daughter were to turn up alive, she would be the true rightful heir; he would not be able to take the full title of the property at this time. However, since it looked like Starleena Diamond would not be found alive, the law firm wanted to take the matter to the courts to have a judge declare Starleena Diamond officially dead.

Mickie gave him a key to one of the trailers on the property that Jaxson had lived in and suggested he visit while she and the law firm took care of the legal details. He thanked her for the information and left the office, his mind racing with thoughts of the commune and his long-lost brother.

Back at his truck, Jax eagerly awaited his return. He was not about to leave Jax alone at the house again, and he had left his vehicle running with the air conditioner on while he was in the attorney's office. As soon as he stepped inside, Jax meowed loudly, demanding answers.

He started the truck and headed towards the commune. He saw the locked chain across the driveway as he reached the entrance. Thankfully, one of the keys Mickie had given him went to the lock.

He drove up to and parked next to the weathered old trailer that his brother had lived in. As he got out, he could feel eyes on him from the residents living in the other trailers and the old house. As he got out and walked up to the door where Jaxson had once lived, he Expected someone to stop him or, at the very least, inquire why he was trespassing, but no one stepped out of their homes.

The trailer's interior was dimly lit, but as his eyes adjusted, He noticed old family pictures hanging around the small living room. He saw pictures of his mother, his two older brothers, and one of the missing Starleena, and, to his surprise, a picture of a younger version of himself. The photo of him was taken when he was about seven years of age, he assumed. He remembered the red and blue jumpsuit his mother had made him wear. He was sitting on his favorite bicycle, smiling brightly. He had no memory of this photo or of ever having met Jaxson.

Exploring the trailer further, Crox stumbled upon a worn-out journal. It belonged to Jaxson Diamond, and as he read the entries, he began learning about the man his brother had been. Jaxson Diamond had been eccentric and deeply connected to the forest, wanting to live off the grid and have nature support him, his common-law wife Analee, and their daughter Starleena.

According to the journal, Analee had a unique gift that allowed her to communicate with this forest Shadow.

This gift made her and the commune members a target. Jaxson believed Starleena's disappearance resulted from Analee's continued involvement with this Shadow. As night fell, he sat by the big window, checking to see if anyone came up to the trailer.

Jax curled up next to him. He felt a strange energy in the air as if the forest was whispering its secrets. He pushed it all out of his mind as he continued reading the journal, hoping for any information to help him find Starleena or locate her body.

The Journal contained no other helpful information, only that he and Analee often fought after Starleena's disappearance. Analee wanted Jaxson to stop going to the forest to look for her. Analee believed Starleena ran away and hitched a ride with someone. Jaxson never thought his daughter would ever run away.

As he read, he felt there was something more to this story than what was written in the journal. There were gaps, and some pages had been ripped out.

He decided to spend the night in the trailer, wanting to immerse himself in the surroundings. He set up a makeshift bed on the couch and tried to get some rest, but the weight of all the information he had uncovered weighed heavily on his mind.

The night wore on; strange sounds echoed through the woods surrounding the property. He could hear the rustling of leaves and occasional animal howls, but something else was unsettling. It was as if the forest was whispering, asking him to come out. Suddenly, Jax stood up, his ears pricked, and his tail fluffed up in alertness. He stared out of the window, fixated on something he could not see.

The black cat let out a growl, a sound he had never heard from him before. It was clear that Jax sensed something dangerous was outside.

"What is it, boy?" he asked, but the cat did not answer. He opened the front door to see what had caught Jax's attention. In the distance, he thought he saw a faint glow, a shimmering light moving between the tall trees.

As the glow grew brighter, He noticed a shadowy figure moving along. The form was hazy and indistinct, like wisps of smoke dancing in the wind. Fear gripped him, and he felt his complete bladder start to release. He caught hold of himself and went to step out the front door when, all of a sudden, he felt pain in his leg from Jax clawing at him. In his mind, he heard Jax say, *No, do not go out there, Danger.* He then let out another growl.

Crox paid no attention. He quickly gathered his belongings, not caring about the mess he left behind in the trailer. He scooped up Jax in his arms, rushed out to his truck, and sped off into the night. As he fled, the glow faded like the forest had swallowed the light.

When he got home, he went straight to bed, feeling scared and exhausted. Jax climbed next to him, a soft purr emanating from him. Thankfully, he had a dreamless night.

As Crox slept, Jax got up and went into the living room, where the ghost of Starleena and Crox's cousin Danny were waiting for him. There was much to discuss.

Starleena looked mournful as she said, "You have to take him back to the forest; I can't stay here long. The Shadow will soon find me." The ghost of Danny Chimed in, "Keep my cousin safe. I'll be watching."Jax bowed his head and said, "*I will do my best.*"

Chapter 6

Death is the Beginning

The following day, Crox woke up feeling a mix of confusion and self-doubt. The craziness of what came out of the forest was enough to drive anyone mad. He still had no idea what came out of those woods. In the morning light, he began to think perhaps it had all been in his imagination.

He felt sad, not knowing he had a brother who lived just a few miles away and that he had never got a chance to know him. However, there were photos of him with Jaxson. Why didn't he remember the picture he saw in Jaxson's home of him as a child?

After he fed Jax and drank a strong cup of coffee, he called Relda to tell her what had transpired over the last couple of days.

Relda told him she had been stressed at work and could not talk until that evening. She suggested they have dinner with Vonda at her home on Honeysuckle Hill.

Since he had some time on his hands, he decided he and Jax would drive down to his office at Crox Home Sales Inc., which wasn't far. The office was located on Charles St. near his favorite ice cream place, Carl's Ice Cream, a local favorite in Fredericksburg since 1947.

He was proud of his little City of Fredericksburg. That is why he chose to live and work here and knew he would also die here.

The office was just as he had left it—organized and running smoothly. Armand, his second in command, was a tall, thin man in his late 40s with wild, busy brown hair and dark brown eyes. Armand was one of those infuriating "cup is half full" type of person. No matter what the problem was, he always found a lesson in it. Armand had been working with Crox for five years and had proven himself to be able to take the reins of the business.

Armand greeted him warmly, surprised to see him at the office. Crox briefly explained that he wanted to catch up on the latest developments in the real estate company's activities. Even though he was semi-retired, he still liked to pop into the office occasionally and do a surprise audit, much to Armand's dismay.

Sitting at his desk, he felt comfortable and familiar. The chaos of the past few days started to fade into the background and out of mind as he immersed himself in the operations updates.

Armand advised him on the various properties they had on the market, recent closed sales, and what community events Crox Home Sales Inc. agents had been involved with. All in all, the business was thriving.

At least there was one thing in his life that was going normally. During his lunch break, he went to Carl's and got an old-fashioned chocolate malt—the perfect treat. He also got his kitty sidekick a small cup of vanilla ice cream. Jax, sitting beside him in the truck, watched curiously as his human sucked down his desert. He felt a semblance of normalcy returning to his life for a brief moment.

Later that evening, he met Relda at Honey SuckleHill, where Vonda greeted them with big hugs and kisses and a large bottle of white wine. Vonda grilled chicken thighs marinated in tequila for dinner and served them with a big salad.

After enjoying the meal on the patio, they changed and got in the hot tub. Crox shared with Relda and Vonda all the strange events that had occurred over the past few days. The chaos Jax caused to his home and, more importantly, the discovery of his half-brother's existence. Vonda listened intently, her eyes full of empathy. Relda just sat stone-faced, taking it all in.

Relda finally broke her silence and said, "This is a lot to process, and I know it must be overwhelming for you. We have a dead man that you're now telling us is your brother and his missing daughter, who is also probably dead. Where the hell is the girl's mother?"

Crox nodded, acknowledging her concern. "I know, Relda. It's fucked up, to say the least."

Vonda chimed in, "Maybe the three of us should visit the commune. I'm sure I can get some tongues to wag." she said with a wink.

"I don't know; this is still an active police investigation. As far as Starleena Diamond is concerned. I shouldn't even have Crox with me while I am investigating officially."

Jax, quietly observing the conversation, said, *"You must go back to the commune. It's the only way to get to the bottom of all this. I can't promise it'll be safe, but I'll be there with you."*

He looked over at Relda and said, "Hun, all three of us are involved now, and if Vonda can help get tongues to loosen up with her sexy ass, I say bring her along. Those living on that commune must know more than they are letting on."

After Vonda provided a few more drinks, they got Relda to change her mind. The next day, Relda and Vonda met at his place and set out for the commune, driving in his truck. Jax rode in the backseat, his eyes alert and focused. They arrived at the entrance to the secluded community and cautiously made their way up the driveway, parking by Jaxson Diamond's trailer, which now was presumably his property.

The atmosphere around the commune was quiet, with not many people milling about. They were soon greeted by a couple of the residents who lived on the property, who seemed to be aware that he was now the perceived owner of their home. Vonda started conversations with a couple of younger men who were tending to a broken fence towards the back of the property near the forest. She tried to gather any information about Starleena Diamond and her mother.

As Vonda chatted with the commune residents, Crox noticed a woman standing in a nearby vegetable garden. The young woman seemed to be observing them intently, her eyes darting between Crox and Relda. Something about her intense demeanor caught his attention, so he grabbed Relda by the arm and walked over to speak with the woman.

"Hello, excuse me," he said gently. I'm Crox, and this is Sheriff Relda Michealson. We're trying to find information about Starleena Diamond and her mother, Analee Morgan. Would you mind if we asked you a couple of questions?"

The woman hesitated for a moment before nodding yes. "I'm Kristen," she said softly. "Nice to meet you."

Kristen appeared to be in her mid-30s, with multi-colored hair. She wore denim overalls. Besides the crazy hair color, Kristen fit right in with the country setting. Though she looked like she had a tough exterior, Crox could tell she was quiet and shy.

Relda asked, "Do you know why StarleenaDiamond left the confines of the property before she went missing? Did she have any issues with her parents or anyone else living here?"

Kristen looked around as if unsure whether to share what she knew. "I don't know all the details, but I have heard rumors." Her eyes darted nervously around and continued when no one was looking in their direction. "Starleena disappeared soon after the teacher we had here at the commune left, Sean Palmer. "He was a newcomer to the commune. Analee brought him here to teach the kids. Everyone had pulled their kids out of public school, and as Analee and Jaxson said, it would be best to home-school the kids. Sean could do it so the parents had time to tend to the property. There was something off about him, you know? He didn't seem to fit in."

Kristen continued, "Analee met him at a coffee shop in Fredericksburg called Hyperion Expresso and invited him to the commune to teach the kids the day she met him. I don't know if he was qualified to be a teacher."

Crox asked Kristen if she knew where the teacher was now.

"I don't know where he went. People whispered that he might have been involved in something shady, but nobody knows for sure. After Sean left, Jaxson urged us not to talk about it, to keep everything hush-hush."

Vonda joined the conversation, asking, "Do you think Jaxson was trying to cover something up or protect Analee?"

Jaxson said it was for the community's safety, but some of us felt he and Analee were protecting themselves more than anything else."

As they continued to talk with Kristen, she mentioned that one person in the commune might know more. His name was Jacob.

Crox and Relda had already met Jacob, and it looked like they would have to have another conversation with the old man. He thanked Kristen for her time. Crox, Relda, and Vonda made their way over to Jacob's place.

As they approached the old man's trailer, they noticed the door was slightly ajar, and the window curtains were drawn shut. It looked like someone was there, but they could not see anyone inside. Crox knocked on the door, but there was no response.

Crox knocked louder on the side of the trailer, asking if anyone was home. After a moment of silence, the door creaked open slowly, revealing Jacob's worried face. He seemed startled to see them.

Reluctantly, Jacob invited them in, closing the door behind them. The room was dimly lit, and the air was heavy with tension. They all took around a small table, and Jacob glanced nervously at Jax.

Relda asked, "What can you tell me about Sean Palmer, the teacher who lived here at the commune." Jacob cleared his throat and swallowed what he assumed was homemade moonshine. "After Sean came, some of the kids started acting strangely. They became withdrawn and distant. I remember seeing him take some of them away, deep into the forest, for strange lessons."

Are you saying he was molesting some of the children?"Relda asked.

Jacob responded, "Oh no, nothing like that. I think it had something to do with teaching kids about witchcraft. He had all these strange books on spell working and necromancy." Relda's eyes narrowed with concern. "Occult practices? That's troubling. Do you know what he was teaching the children?"

Jacob hesitated before answering, "I don't have all the details, but I overheard him talking about rituals, summoning spirits, and tapping into the energies of nature. It all sounded a bit bizarre, and honestly, I was too scared to get too close to him or the kids when they were with him."

They could see the fear in Jacob's eyes. Relda leaned forward, "Jacob, we need to know everything you know about Sean Palmer. It's crucial to the investigation. If there's any connection between Sean, Starleena, and Analee's disappearance, we must fully understand their relationship."

Jacob's fingers tightened around the glass, his knuckles turning white as he lifted it to his lips. He took a long, deliberate swallow. His eyes closed briefly, and he appeared lost in thought before continuing his story. "After Starleena disappeared, things changed around here. The members of our group became even more secretive, and Jaxson started becoming more distant, almost like he was afraid of something. I tried asking him about it, but he just shut me out."

Vonda, who had been quietly listening, asked, "What about Analee? Did she practice witchcraft with Sean?"

"I don't know what they did together; I hardly ever saw them hanging out. One night, though, when Sean came out of the woods with Starleena, and Analee confronted him, they argued over a book Starleena was carrying." Jacob answered.

"What kind of book?" Asked Relda

"I don't rightly know. But I heard Analee mention the name of the book, *Death is the Beginning*." Jacob responded.

Jacob's expression turned solemn. "Analee was deeply affected by her daughter's disappearance. She spent days looking for Starleena on her own. Then, one day, Analee just vanished too, not long after Jaxson was found dead in those woods off of Ramouth Church Road. We haven't seen or heard from her since."

Relda nodded understandingly. "You have been very helpful, and we appreciate your assistance. If you remember anything else, please call me anytime."

Back at the truck, the three of them discussed their next steps. Relda suggested another visit to Galinda, the Good Witch: Books, Curiosities, and Notions.

Three humans and one feline headed out of Stafford County and back to Fredericksburg. They rode in silence, except the feline. Jax started having a lively conversation with Starleena's ghost as they made their way to Caroline Street in downtown Fredericksburg.

Starleena was irritated. "You have to find Mom. Please hurry, find the book. It has the power to release me and the others from the Shadow."

When the crew arrived at the bookshop, they saw it was closed up tight. No light could be seen through the front window, and they saw no movement inside. Relda knocked loudly, but no one came to the door. " Well, this was a waste of time," Vonda said.

"Perhaps not." He said, "Who wants a cup of coffee on me? Hyperion Espresso is just up the block."

Relda and Vonda agreed to the coffee. There is nothing wrong with a caffeine high. As they walked to Hyperion Espresso, He thought they might discover more about Sean Palmer since he and Analee supposedly met at this coffee shop.

As they entered the coffee shop, the aroma of freshly brewed coffee filled the air. They found a corner table and settled down with their drinks. Vonda made sure to hide Jax in her big oversized purse. The three sat in silence, drinking their fancy coffees.

Crox got up to order another cup of coffee. While he waited, he asked the barista if she had ever had a customer named Sean Palmer.

The barista, a friendly young woman with a bright smile, paused momentarily. "Sean Palmer?" she said, "Yeah, I remember him. He often came in here, always sitting in that corner booth over there." She pointed to a spot near the back of the coffee shop.

The barista leaned in slightly, lowering her voice. "Sean was a peculiar guy, that's for sure," she said. He seemed nice enough, but there was something off about him. He used to sit alone, reading old books, and sometimes, he'd sketch some strange symbols on the napkins."

"Did you ever see him with a book called *Death is the Beginning*?" He asked. The barista shook her head. "I can't recall."He then asked if he had been in recently. "Not in months. He used to come in at least twice a week, but I haven't seen him in months."

As he continued his conversation with the barista, Vonda could not help but notice that some of the other customers in the coffee shop were glancing in their direction with curious expressions. It appeared Jax had gotten out of her purse and was sitting under the table, listening to the conversation.

The barista then asked them to please leave. Cats aren't allowed in the coffee shop.

Once back at the truck, Relda said, "Hey, let's return to your place. I want to get my car. I will stop at the Sheriff's office to see what I can find out about Sean's background."

Crox looked in the backseat at Jax, his green eyes filled with concern. *I felt a presence;* Crox heard the cat say his mind.

"What is it?" He answered back telepathically.

I don't know; I can't see it but only feel a strong presence of something dark calling for you.

As he drove off, Crox thought to himself, "Well, shit in the bucket, I am finally going insane."

Vonda and Relda were utterly oblivious to this conversation between Crox and Jax.

Chapter 7

DESTINY

The truck's atmosphere was tense. Jax's warning about a dark presence had him on edge, and the mystery surrounding Sean Palmer only deepened after the conversation with the Barista from Hyperion Espresso.

Once they arrived back at his home, they agreed to meet back at the Sheriff's office later that evening. Relda and Vonda did not hang around; both women seemed to want to get away from him. Once alone, he decided to get some fresh air and walked around his neighborhood, with Jax following close behind.

As they strolled through a walking path behind the house, the feeling that they were being watched spooked him. The woods surrounding the trail seemed to have eyes. Jax kept his senses alert, occasionally looking over his shoulder, his fur along his tail bushed out; he could not pinpoint the source of the ominous presence felt, but it was there nonetheless.

He was sure someone or something was watching their every move, which was unnerving. He began to feel unsafe, even in his neighborhood.

Meanwhile, Relda arrived at the Sheriff's office and began poring over police records to see if anything regarding Sean Palmer was on file.

Relda soon discovered a history of minor criminal offenses, but he had maintained a low profile over the years. The most notable incident was a petty theft charge a few years back.

As she continued searching, Relda learned that Analee Morgan, Starleena's mother, had no criminal record. By all accounts, she was a relatively quiet and ordinary woman. She had worked at Galinda the Good Witch: Books, Curiosities, and Notions for at least a year before she left town.

Relda contacted colleagues in neighboring counties to see if they had any leads on Sean Palmer or Analee Morgan.

Vonda was waiting for them when he and Jax returned to his house. She had been on his laptop, trying to find any dirt on Sean, Analee, or Jaxson. Vonda was known for her ability to dig up information on almost anyone.

Vonda shared what she had found as they sat in the living room. It turned out that Sean Palmer had a somewhat shady past. He had been involved in several new-age spiritual groups, some known to dabble in dark magic. "There were whispers of him being associated with a group called"The Circle of EternalShadows."

"The Circle of the Eternal Shadow?" Crox repeated with a furrowed brow. "That sounds like some straight-up foolishness."

"It does, "Vonda agreed, "but they were real enough, at least to some extent. I can't find much on them; they are a pretty secretive group."

He sighed, feeling the weight of all this craziness pressing down on him. "We need more information on these people," he said. "We can't afford to be in the dark, especially if there's a connection with Starleena's disappearance."

Vonda decided she had enough of this game, as she called it. She bid him a farewell, and off she left, headed back to Honey Suckle Hill.

Crox sat back on the couch and thought. A secret group, The Circle of Eternal Shadows. It was almost laughable.

Jax joined him on the couch, settling in his lap, a soft purr initiated by the small cat.

Soon, he found himself asleep, and a nightmare was upon him. He was back in the forest of Ramouth Church Road, trapped in the wreckage of his car. This was more than a dream; it seemed like a memory.

Lucky, the cat, came to him, jarring him back to consciousness from licking the blood on his forehead. However, this time, he heard voices from behind him; he was unable to turn to see who the owners of these voices were.

He heard a female voice say, "He belongs to the Shadow, take him."

He heard a male voice, "No, that is Pittapat's only son; the Shadow can have him."

The female voice said, " He has entered the Shadow'srealm, and it will feed on him."

"No," came the man's voice, "I will not allow this to happen.

This man belongs to the Circle of Eternal Shadows."

The female voice angrily yelled, "She is long dead and is no longer our High Priestess. Neither she nor her bloodline has any powers over the Shadow." Crox felt a chill run down his spine as he listened to the argument.

Crox desperately tried to turn around to see who was speaking, but his body remained stuck in the twisted metal of the car, just as it had been that fateful day when he had his accident.

The voices continued, their words now echoing in his mind. The male voice spoke again, "We must protect him. If the Shadow finds him, it will trap his soul, and he may be the only one now who can control the Shadow, using the Book."

The female voice coldly said, "Just because his mother wrote the book and was able to use it to control the Shadow, he knows nothing of its power or how to use it; the power of Death is the Beginning died with his mother."

As the dream continued, he saw a shadowy figure emerge from the darkness, its form twisted and contorted. I reached out with shadowy arms, attempting to embrace him.

Fear gripped him as he struggled to break free from the car wreckage, desperate to escape the approaching darkness. He could feel the cold grip of the shadow inching closer, overwhelming his mind. Just as it seemed like the darkness would consume him, he awoke with Jax standing on his chest.

When he awoke, the last thing he remembered from the dream was a voice saying, "He was meant for the Shadow; you have changed his destiny."

Crox sat up in a cold sweat, his heart pounding in his chest. He looked around, relieved to be back in his living room, safe from the haunting dream.

What in the world was that all about, Crox thought. He had not thought of his mother for some time; could she be somehow a part of this? He had not seen her since the accident; they hadn't been that close.

Crox didn't even know she had remarried and had another son. So why would he know if she was a part of some cult and she had written a devil magic book?

What did it mean in the dream that his destiny had changed? What destiny? He decided to call Relda instead of meeting her at the Sheriff's office. He was too exhausted to drive. As Crox dialed her number, he hoped she could find some information about his mother and this mysterious Circle of the Eternal Shadow.

Relda picked up the call, and he quickly recounted the details of his dream. Relda listened intently and told him she would look into possible connections between his mother and the Circle of the Eternal Shadow occult group.

Crox went to the bathroom to splash some water on his face. Looking up in the mirror, he saw Starleena looking back at him. Her face contorted in anger, and then she was gone.

He struck the mirror with his fist, shattering it, and yelled, "I am getting pretty fucking tired of this shit."

Jax came running into the bathroom, his eyes full of fear. Then, in his mind, he heard, *"Your destiny now is to find the book* Death is the Beginning. *You will know what to do and when to see it."*

"What does that mean, Jax?" Crox whispered, more to himself than to the cat.

Jax blinked but said no more, turned and left the room. His mind raced with questions about his mother and the Circle of Eternal Shadows, and it seemed like each new discovery only led to more confusion.

Crox decided this would all have to wait until tomorrow. He would order some Chinese food, veg out watching Netflix, and let his mind go blank. He chose to watch *The Exorcist*. Not a wise choice, Jax thought.

Late in the night, he was awakened by a strange noise. Crox got up and walked into the living room. He saw a person standing there dressed in all black. He could not tell if it was a man or a woman in the dim light. Crox yelled, "Who are you?" and rushed forward.

The stranger brandished a handgun, stopping him in his tracks. The Stanger slowly walked towards the door, never taking the gun off. Then Jax walked into the room, and the stranger tensed and turned the gun on the cat, pulling the trigger. Three shots rang out, one hitting Jax and throwing the little cat backward into the kitchen.

Crox rushed forward, but the stranger bolted out the front door into the night before he had a chance to catch them.

He quickly scooped up Jax, who whimpered in pain, and rushed him to Saint Frances Animal Hospital, which was thankfully only two miles away on Harrison Road. They had 24-hour emergency care.

The veterinarian and pet tech worked tirelessly to save Jax's life, and thankfully, the bullet missed all his vital organs. Despite the trauma, Jax was expected to recover.

Relda arrived at the animal hospital with another sheriff to take his statement, and she advised she already had an officer at his house taking photos and searching for fingerprints.

Crox told Relda, "The intruder had deliberately shot Jax, but why? It's not like he was a guard dog.

The Vet informed him that he would need to stay at the animal hospital for at least a week or so to recover. He walked into the back, where they had Jax sedated. He bent down and kissed the cat on the head as a tear rolled down his cheek. He was becoming quite bonded with the feline.

Crox returned to Hyperion Espresso, where Relda met him and ordered a tall double-shot expresso for them both. The caffeine would do them both a great deal of good.

As they sipped their coffee, Relda told him what she had found out about his mother, Pittapat. "Your mom has no other marriage certificate on file, other than when she was married to your father, although there is a birth record where she gave birth to one Jaxson Diamond eight years after you were born." He sat there stunned.

He had no memory of his mother being pregnant when he was eight, though he was bounced around a lot between family members when he was growing up. He thought again of the photo of him and Jaxson. Why did he have no memory of him?

Relda mentioned that there was no record of the Circle of Eternal Shadows. "If your mom was with some cult, it was all on the down low." He thought everything his mother did seemed to be on the down low. He got up to leave, giving Relda a strong hug and thanking her for being there for him.

Relda invited him to stay with her for a few days or until they caught the person who broke in. He rejected the offer, telling her no one was going to chase him out of his home. He would just keep his .38 special close by.

Relda called out. "Funny. How did one event change your life? Do you think these life-changing moments are all laid out in our Destiny?"

Crox shrugged his shoulders as he walked out. However, his mind hung on the word "Destiny. What was his destiny?"

Over the next few days, he split his time between visiting Jax and digging through boxes from the attic of old photos and letters that belonged to his mother and that he had stored after her death.

In one album, he came across a photo of himself from grade school, and it looked as if something was behind it; Crox pulled the plastic sheet that held the photo, and the letter addressed to him by his mother fell out.

My Dearest Son,

If you are reading this, it means I am dead. I've made many mistakes along the way in this life. You were always the light of my life, even though I couldn't always be there for you. I leave you a book I wrote many years ago. It is called Death is the Beginning. *This book will explain more about your destiny. Use it carefully. I beg of you, never go near Rammouth Church Road or the woods near it. It is not safe for you, and the book will explain more. If anyone ever approaches you with a group called "Circle of the Eternal Shadow," I want you to run and get away from them as quickly as possible. They are dangerous people.*

Know my spirit is with you always, Mom

His hands trembled as he read his mother's swords. Crox carefully placed the letter back in its sleeve and stared at his old photograph, unsure what to do next.

His mother's letter did not share the location of the book *Death is the Beginning*. Where could it be? He suddenly thought of someone who knew of old occult books: " Sun—Moon," the owner of Galinda the Good Witch: Books, Curiosities, and Notions.

He decided to pay another visit to Sun-Moon, either at her shop or home.

Meanwhile, Relda had been busy, too, tirelessly following leads and investigating every possible angle on the person who broke into his home and shot Jax. She had discovered a latent fingerprint on the back kitchen window. The break-in wasn't random, as the fingerprint belonged to Sean Palmer.

Relda dispatched officers to Sean Palmer's last known address. Relda called Crox and updated him on the situation with Sean.

Relda told Crox that officers were currently at Sean's last known address and that she hoped to find some leads or clues there. Relda also urged him to be careful. Sean Plamer could be anywhere, and he was to be considered armed and extremely dangerous.

Crox hung up the phone, his mind racing. Who was this Sean Palmer, and what was he looking for? Also, did he have a connection to the Circle of Eternal Shadows? The group his mother had warned him about in her letter, where they after her book? He remembered what Jax and Relda had said before he left. Was his Destiny to find his mother's book and potentially use it to combat the Shadow?

Chapter 8
Who to Trust?

Crox slept throughout the night during the following days. No strange dreams disturbed his sleep. Jax was healing fast and would be able to come back home within the next few days. Thankfully, nothing weird or out of the ordinary occurred following the night of the break-in and shooting, allowing him to concentrate on Jax's recovery.

In between trips to the veterinary Hospital, he researched online but could not find any other information on his mother or the Circle of Eternal Shadows. He also rechecked the boxes he had stored in the attic but again found nothing of value.

Crox prepared himself mentally for another visit to Sun-Moon, the owner of Galinda the Good Witch: Books, Curiosities, and Notions again. He felt strongly that the shop owner would have some additional information she had not given freely.

Not only did Sun-Moon own the only occult shop in the area, but the way she looked and spoke to him was almost intimate.

Relda had been out of commission during this time; she was investigating both the break-in and shooting, as well as exploring the murder of a young girl whose body had been found under the Falmouth Bridge, floating in the Rappahannock River.

He decided not to wait on her; he would go see Sun-Moon alone. She would be willing to give him more information without a police officer present.

As he drove downtown to the occult store, he felt a vibration in the back of his head, not quite a headache; he wondered if this was some warning not to go back to see the shop owner. On Caroline Street, he could park right in front of the store, which he took as a good sign. The store was closed, though, in his gut, he knew Sun-Moon was inside. He looked up at that strange symbol of the cat with horns over the doorway and wondered why it made him feel dread. He shook off the feeling; he had to keep his wits about him.

Crox was ready to face his destiny, whatever it was, and in his heart, he felt Sun-Moon was a part of it.

He banged loudly on the door until he finally heard a voice yell, "Stop all that damn racket and come in; the doors open."

As he entered the shop, a soft chime announced his arrival. The interior was filled with a different incense smell, more intense than the smell the last time he had been there. It burned the back of his throat.

"Hello?" he called out, but there was no response. He walked further into the shop, his steps creaking on the old wooden floor. As he moved further toward the back of the shop, he noticed a dim light glowing, leading him toward an open doorway.

There, in a dimly lit backroom, sat Sun-Moon. "Welcome, come in," she said, her voice soft and icy. I have been expecting you."

He was taken aback. "You knew I was coming?"

"I know many things," Sun-Moon replied with a condescending smile.

Crox's heart raced as he stood facing her. An overwhelming feeling of intrigue, with a touch of hate for this woman he did not even know, took over him.

Sun-Moon sat at a small table and motioned for him to sit across from her. Despite wanting to stand over her, he obliged her request, trying to suppress his feelings. There was something peculiar about this woman.

"I knew you would come to me again," Sun-Moon said, her dark eyes seemingly peering into his soul. "You have many questions, but are you ready for the answers?

Crox took a deep breath, trying to compose himself. "Yes, I do have a few questions for you. I need to know what if any, information you have on a group called the Circle of the Eternal Shadow and a book called *Death is the Beginning*."

Sun-Moon nodded, her expression unreadable. "Did you know that your late Mother had been a mighty woman, Crox? Are you aware of that?"

He was stunned." How do you know my mother?

"Ah, Ms. Pittapat, I knew her well," Sun-Moon stated slyly.

His eyes widened in shock. "HOW!" Crox shouted in anger."

Watch yourself, boy, do not disrespect me in my place," Sun-Moon replied in an infuriatingly calm voice.

Crox took a deep breath, trying to rein in his emotions before he asked in a more polite tone.

"Okay, fine," he said, "You knew my mother. Tell me everything you know about her, as well as anything you know about the Circle of the Eternal Shadow and a book called *Death is* the Beginning. Please."

Sun-Moon studied him for a moment before speaking. "Your Mother, Pittapat, was a practitioner of witchcraft and a seer of spirits. She was also a high priestess of the Circle of Eternal Shadows. This pagan group was involved in all types of witchcraft, even the black arts. The Circle sought to harness and control the power of the Shadow that dwells in the forest. Pittapa was a small but mighty woman who controlled the circle with an iron fist."

Sun-Moon continued. "But power has its price, and the dark arts she practiced eventually consumed her. The Circle of Eternal Shadows is an old organization that has existed for over a century, with members all over this region. The first high priestess was Victoria Parham. She and her husband, Shane, came to Stafford County after being run out of Kentucky. It is said Victoria killed her brother-in-law, Ken Parham, when he accused her of being a witch and killed his cotton crops."

Crox interrupted, "What does this have to do with my mother?"

"I'm getting there; hold your tongue." Sun-Moon said as she continued her story, "When they arrived in Stafford, Victoria and Shane built a house near Ramouth Church Road in the forest. Soon after, they started a church called the Circle of Faith, but it never had more than a dozen or so parishioners, and it soon shut down. It wasn't too long after rumors around town started that the group, who now went by the Circle of the Eternal Shadow, was practicing witchcraft in the woods." -

Sun-Moon continued, "One night, the family disappeared without a trace; members of the Circle said they had gone camping and may have been attacked by a bear, but nothing ever was located, no camping gear or any other physical evidence of the family. The group's leaders were gone. However, the Circle of the Eternal Shadow remained. Eventually, your mother became their High Priestess."

Crox thought his mother had always been on the move, and he never got close to her as a child; she was very secretive even then. But to be a high priestess of an occult religious group was a bit much to comprehend.

"What about a book called *Death is the Beginning*?" He asked, his voice cracking slightly.

Sun-Moon's eyes narrowed as she leaned in closer, her voice dropping to a whisper. "Ah, *Death is the Beginning*, a book of great power. Did you know that your mother wrote it with the help of old magical spells she had collected over the years? It is said to hold the secrets of Life and Death, the boundaries between this world and the next. Whoever possesses it can wield the power to trap or release a person's soul."

"I need to find this book. Do you know where it is?"

Sun-Moon chuckled darkly. "Oh, my dear man, do you truly think you can handle such power? The path you're embarking on can only lead to your death."

"That is my choice; now tell me where the book is," Crox demanded. Sun-Moon responded, "I do not know where the book ended up after Pittapat's Death; I am sure others are seeking *Death is the Beginning*, and they will stop at nothing to get their hands on it.

Be cautious of whom you trust; anyone in your life could be a Circle of the Eternal Shadow member and may use you to get to the book."

"Thanks for the advice, considering I don't even trust you," Crox stated dryly.

Sun-Moon sighed. "Very well. Take this, though," she said, handing him a small pendant on a gold chain featuring a cat with horns. "It will offer you some protection. Keep it close at all times." Crox hesitated before he reached out and took the pendant, feeling its weight in his hand.

Crox left the shop and headed over to Saint Frances Animal Hospital to visit with Jax.

Jax was up and about, and he could take him to a small room and spend some time alone with his feline companion.

"How are you doing, little one?" Crox asked

Jax looked up at him and purred softly, but no words came. He wondered if Jax had lost his ability to communicate with him.

With Jax sitting on his lap and Jax Purring softly, he felt again a sense of comfort just being with the feline. Even though the cat was not talking, his presence was reassuring.

After leaving the vet hospital, he decided to stop by the Sheriff's office to update Relda on what he had learned from Sun-Moon. The Sheriff's office was full of activity, so Relda took him back to her office to talk. He showed her the pendant and told her what Sun-Monn had said about his mother's involvement with the Circle of Eternal Shadows.

Relda listened carefully, her eyes focused on his words. "It's clear there's more to this than we initially thought. We need to keep digging and find out if this group, the Circle of the Eternal Shadow, has a connection to Analee Morgan or Starleena's disappearance?"

Relda then filled him in on the case of the dead girl found underneath the Falmouth Bridge. She had discovered a possible connection between the break-in at his home and the murder of this young girl.

The girl had no identification, but she did have a Visa credit card in her back pocket in the name of Sean Palmer. The investigation was underway, and Relda had officers out talking to the locals who lived near the bridge. She had also sent the dead girls' fingerprints to the FBI at Quantico.

Crox left the police station and, since he had nothing else to do, decided to hit the ABC liquor store and pick up a fifth of Jack Daniels. Then, he made his way to Sunset Memorial Gardens cemetery to visit his mother's grave.

When he arrived at the cemetery, Crox knew precisely where to go. He had buried his mother next to the pet cemetery, though he had tried to get the cemetery to allow him to bury Pittapat in the pet area, as she had loved her cats immensely. This was not allowed, so he got her as close to the pet area of the graveyard as he could.

Crox settled down on the ground at his mother's grave. He then took out the bottle of Jack Daniels took a big swig from the bottle, and poured some on the grave. "Shalom," he said

Looking at his mother's headstone, which he had bought, Crox noticed a couple of added features that he had not put on it. One was the saying, *"Death is the Beginning,"* and next to it was the symbol of the cat with horns.

He was infuriated that his mother's grave had been desecrated.

Crox got up, brushed the dirt off his pants, and started to walk back to his truck when he saw Vonda approaching him. What was she doing there, he thought?

He realized she had not seen him yet, so he quickly hid behind some tall bushes and observed her. Vonda placed flowers on his mother's grave. It looked like she was talking, but Crox could not hear what she was saying. He soon realized she wasn't talking but singing—or perhaps chanting.

Vonda must have felt his presence as she turned in his direction.

"What are you doing here?" He asked

Vonda's face was calm, and her voice was level when she replied, "I was just paying my respects; it's what Pittapat would have wanted."

He didn't believe her for a second. " Is that all, or are you following me, perhaps looking for a book?"

Vonda chuckled darkly. "Ah yes, the book *Death is the Beginning*. If you have it, I suggest you give it to me; I can put it to better use than you can."

He was stunned and confused. Is Vondaa part of the Circle of Eternal Shadows? Is she a witch? He thought. He had so many questions.

Vonda interrupted his thoughts, "I will go now, but I suggest you be careful with whom you trust; there are people in this town who would do anything to get their hands on that book."

Vonda started walking away, and he said, " Wait—what do you have to do with my mother and the book *Death is the Beginning*?"

Vonda turned and smiled. " I knew your mother long before I met you; why do you think I made sure to become friends with you? I always knew you would eventually lead me to the book."

"I don't have it," Croxed stated.

"Not yet, but you will have it soon," Vonda replied.

Vonda Turned to walk away. Crox watched her disappear between the headstones. Then he turned and looked back at his mother's gravesite. He just stood there, not knowing what to do.

Crox wondered, was his friendship with Vonda all these years a farce? Tears welled up in his eyes at the thought of being used.

Crox was beginning to think the only person he could trust was his new cat.

Sun-Moon was right. He had to be careful with who he trusted. He thought he had an ally in Vonda, but her wanting to get her hands on the book made him question everyone in his life now. Who else in his Circle of friends was a member of this cult? Who could he rely on?

At least he knew one thing: the book was causing chaos, and he had to find it before some member of this cult group did. He also needed to determine whether this book could help find Starleena or her body.

Crox looked at the sky and said a final goodbye to his mother.

Driving home, his mind swirled with thoughts and emotions. He needed to process everything he had learned from Sun-Moon and confront the reality that his mother had been involved with the Circle of the Eternal Shadow and even had authored this book so many people wanted. Not to mention coming to terms with Vonda's betrayal. And what of Relda? Could she still be trusted?

Upon reaching his house, he found Relda sitting on the front porch waiting for him. He decided to keep to himself what had happened over the past few hours. He would have to find out if Relda could still be trusted.

He invited Relda inside and suggested they have a drink and catch up. He then asked Relda if the Sheriff's office had any leads on Sean Palmer.

"None so far."She stated.

Relda also advised that she had dug into the history of the Circle of Eternal Shadows, and it seems like they may have been connected to a few unsolved disappearances over the years. He listened intently.

"People have whispered about the Circle's involvement, but there never has been any concrete evidence of this occult group's existence," Relda stated

"How has it stayed off the police radar until now?" Crox asked

"There are hundreds of missing person reports in our region every year, and if this cult group is as secretive as believed, they must operate below the radar," Relda explained. " They also may have connections that help them avoid detection.

Chapter 9

Girl Under the Bridge

Crox tossed and turned in his bed, his body soaked in a cold sweat, as he dreamed. He was with his cousin Danny, but they were not at the large Oak tree in the grassy meadow, which was the usual location whenever his cousin came to him in dreams. This time, he was in a dark tunnel. Danny was frantic, pulling him along. Crox could sense his cousin's fear.

Stumbling through the dark tunnel, Crox noticed a faint glow ahead of them. Danny's grip tightened on his arm, urging him to move faster. The fear in Danny's eyes was undeniable, and it fueled his sense of urgency.

"Danny, what's going on? where are we going?" Crox asked, trying to keep up with Danny's hurried pace.

"We don't have much time; move your ass, Cuz. We have to reach Sherry."

The endless tunnel felt damp and cold, the walls expanding with every step they took. Crox's heart beat painfully in his chest, and the sound of their footsteps echoed loudly in his ears.

As they ran, the glow ahead intensified, and they finally reached the end of the tunnel. They emerged, a river in front of them. The rapids thundered as the water poured down a large waterfall downstream.

Danny grabbed his arm and whispered, "Look yonderCuz, do you see her?"

He squinted through the darkness, barely making out the figure in the distance.

A little girl stood at the edge of the river. Anny pulled her closer to better see her features. he was a small child with long blond hair. He was wearing jeans and a bright pink T-shirt. He also had on sparkly flip-flops.

He immediately knew who she was, even though he had never seen her. It's Sherry," he uttered under his breath.

Danny tightened his grip and nodded before cautiously approaching the little girl.

As they approached, he could feel an icy chill settling over them, and his fear grew more intense. The little girl seemed so fragile, and he wanted to protect her.

Danny stepped forward and cautiously asked, "Sherry, what are you doing here, sweetheart?"

The little girl just stared at him, her large eyes full of terror. Then, out of nowhere, a shadowy figure emerged; it embraced Sherry, and they both vanished.

Crox awoke with a start, a cold shiver running down his spine. He quickly reached for his phone to check the time. It was 3:20 A.M., and his bed was soaked from his sweat.

Crox lay there, scrolling through the news on his phone. He saw a headline: "Girl Found Dead in the Rappahannock River, Under the Falmouth Bridge, has been identified as missing Fredericksburg resident, Sherry Shew: Sheriff Relda Michealson is leading investigation."

The dream could not have been a mere coincidence. Crox promised himself to call Relda as soon as the sun rose; he wanted to learn more about little Sherry and her investigation. But before that, he had to pick up Jax from the animal hospital where he had been recovering. The bill for his care would be astronomical, and he dreaded seeing the final amount. Despite this, he gathered his resolve and went to Saint Frances Animal Hospital to collect Jax and pay the whopping $3500 bill. As he carried Jax out, he was relieved that his familiar had healed completely.

Crox spent the day at home, giving Jax all the attention and care he could. Jax did not speak to him as the cat sat on the couch, purring contently beside him. As he petted Jax, his mind wandered back to last night's dream. The mention of Sherry Shew on the morning news was troubling. He knew he had to talk to Relda about this. It seemed to be more than just a coincidence. He openly spoke of this, hoping Jax would chime in, but to no avail.

Throughout the day, Crox could not shake the feeling that his dreams were trying to tell him something. The coincidence of dreaming about Sherry, who was the same girl found dead, was haunting him. Crox leaned back onto the couch, exhaustion taking over his body. He looked at Jax, hoping the cat could help him understand everything, but Jax remained silent. It was going to be a long night.

Crox decided to call on a friend he had not seen in some time, Pastor Carrie Seal. She led the congregation at Fredericksburg's 1st Pentecostal Church.

Pastor Seal was not your typical religious leader. Before the church's calling, she was the lead singer in Night Breeders, a heavy metal rock band.

She was a tiny woman with long black curly hair with a white strip down the middle. She also still had a sailor's dirty mouth. Pastor Carrie Seal had earned a Ph. D. in occult studies, so he thought she might be able to shed some light on the Eternal Circle of Shadow.

Pastor Seal answered the phone. Excitement and nervousness bubbled within him. He hoped Carrie would be open-minded enough to believe his story. He quickly explained what had happened over the past few days and his dream about little Sherry. He also told Pastor Seal what he had on the Circle of the Eternal Shadow. He waited a few moments with bated breath for the pastor's response.

"Ah, the Circle of the Eternal Shadow," the pastor began. I have heard of them. They are local and have been around for about a century or so. They are known to practice dark witchcraft."

"Do you think you can help? We can do some research together," Crox suggested.

"Yes, let's do that. We should meet soon. Gather your information together, and I'll pull what the church archives have. We'll figure out a plan from there," Pastor Seal responded.

Crox sighed heavily as the magnitude of the situation finally set in. He did not know what he was getting himself into. Crox had a feeling that things were going to get dangerous.

As Crox stared into the distance, he noticed a reflection from the corner of his eye. He turned and looked at Jax, who was now looking right back at him. The cat seemed to have been studying him for some time, his large emerald green eyes full of unspoken knowledge. Then, in his mind, Crox heard Jax say, *"The Shadow caused Sherry's death."*

"How?" Crox asked.

You will see. came the cat's cryptic reply

Crox sent Relda a text, "Please contact me ASAP."

Relda responded to his text, promising to meet him first thing in the morning. The tension kept him awake throughout the night. At least if he couldn't sleep, he wouldn't dream.

The following day, Relda arrived looking weary. She explained that the investigation into Sherry Shew's death was ongoing and may be connected to Sean Palmer. Sherry's family had been devastated, and the Fredericksburg region was on edge.

Pastor Carrie Seal joined them later in the day, bringing with her texts related to the occult but none directly of the Circle of the Eternal Shadow. She added valuable insights into the history and practices of the dark arts, which he found interesting. Still, he was not sure how it all would tie into the dead girl Sherry or the missing Starleena, as well as his mother's involvement with a cult.

As they continued their discussion, Pastor Seal suggested performing a ritual from a spell book she had found to gain insight into his dreams and the connection to the Circle of the Eternal Shadow. She believed that tapping into the spiritual realm might offer clues and answers.

"What!" Relda exclaimed. "I thought you were a woman of God. What do you know of occult practices?"

In a low, patient voice, Pastor Seal responded, "Where there is light, there is dark. If you wish to be in the light, sometimes you must go through the dark."

Relda sat back and huffed under her breath.

"I'm willing to do whatever I can to learn about this occult group and find my mother's book," Crox stated firmly.

Relda piped up, "Let's not forget we have a possible killer on our hands. Sean Palmer is still on the loose."

Pastor Seal arranged some white candles and a portrait of the Virgin Mary on the coffee table to create a makeshift altar. She explained that it was a safe place to call upon spirits from the other side to cross over.

Pastor Carrie Seal began the ritual with a prayer for protection and guidance, asking for the spirits of light to surround them. She then instructed Crox to close his eyes, take deep breaths, and focus on the dreams he had been experiencing. She then had him drink a dark, chalky-tasting drink she presented from her pocket.

As Crox followed the instructions, he felt a strange sensation come over him. It was as if he was floating above his body, watching the scene unfold below him. Crox saw young Sherry Shew running from someone or something in a dark tunnel. He felt her terror as she ran, running toward a light shining from up ahead.

Suddenly, the scene changed. Crox now saw Sherry standing by the river bank and the shadowy figure embracing her before they disappeared, the same as in his dreams. It was as if he was reliving the scene. Then, from out of nowhere, Sherry's mangled body lay before him, and the Shadow was at his side. Pastor Seal was also there with him. She instructed him, "Ask questions, seek answers," she whispered.

"What are you? What do you want?" Crox asked the shadowy figure.

The figure turned toward him, its face obscured by darkness. Crox could feel its evil essence. It spoke in a chilling, hollow voice, "Your Soul, you belong to me."

Pastor Seal stepped between Crox and the Shadow.

"Leave this place, dark entity! You have no power here!" she declared with authority. The words seemed to echo in this dream realm, and the shadowy figure recoiled momentarily.

Crox felt a rush of strength and protection wash over him, coming from Pastor Seal's presence. This helped him muster the courage to ask the Shadow, "Where is Starleena Diamond?"

The dark figure sneered, "You belong to me. I will not stop until you are mine." In an instant, the communication was cut off. Crox collapsed to the ground, huddled in a ball and sobbing uncontrollably.

Relda and Pastor Seal helped him up and walked him over to the couch.

"What the hell was that, Carrie?" Crox cried out.

"I'm not sure, but I will help you fight it." She Responded.

Relda, looking confused, asked, "What the hell just happened."

Pastor Seal attempted to explain to Relda the dream state she could induce Crox and herself into, which took them into the Shadows' realm. The Shadow was responsible for little Sherry's death.

Relda went red and, in a rage, she shouted," This is all bull shit, a human being, who is most likely Sean Palmer, killed Sherry Shew, not to mention shot your cat! I am tired of all this hocus pocus. I have a murder to solve." She then stormed out, slamming the door behind her.

Crox and Carrie were left stunned by Relda's outburst.

Pastor Seal put a comforting hand on his shoulder. "I understand this is a lot to take in, and it is understandable Relda is skeptical."

Pastor Seal suggested they gather more information on the Circle of the Eternal Shadow occult group and its practices since they were most likely linked to this Shadow creature. We need to fully understand what we are dealing with. She also suggested seeking guidance from other experts in the occult who might have dealt with similar situations.

Crox suggested they get together in a couple of days and go from there.

Pastor Seal agreed and left to head back to her church.

Jax walked into the living room from his spot on the kitchen floor, where he had been worshiping the sun. "Hey there, little one, what's shaking?" Crox asked

Jax looked at him and shook his head. *"Why did you bring that woman here? You are making things worse,"* he heard in his mind.

Jax looked at him with an air of annoyance before saying, *You do not know who is in the Circle of the Eternal Shadow. I am sure They think you have mother's Grimoire, or you know where it is. You need to be cautious. Trust no one but yourself and those who have proven their loyalty to you. The Circle members are watching, and they'll use any weakness they can find*, Jax warned.

"Who killed Sherry Shew? Who?" Crox asked desperation in his voice. Jax went silent and walked out of the room. "Damn You, Cat," Crox yelled out.

Frustratedly, he grabbed a bottle of Jack Daniels and headed to his back deck. He shut the door to keep Jax from coming outside, as he wanted to be alone.

After several hours, he returned inside to find several missed calls and text messages from Relda.

The last text was "CALL ME NOW...WHERE THE HELL ARE YOU?"

Crox immediately called Relda's cell phone, and when she picked up, she blurted out, "Carrie Seal is dead."

"Huh" was the only response he could muster.

"Her car struck a parked car at a high rate of speed on Princess Anne Street. There were no skidmarks, which means she may have fallen asleep at the wheel." Relda stated.

Crox released his grip on the phone and watched it tumble to the floor. He then collapsed, letting out a sigh of despair as everything went black.

Jax walked over to the unconscious man and curled up beside him. Small tears welled up in the eyes as they began to purr softly. The cat wondered, "How many more deaths would there be before his task is done?

Chapter 10

SUSPECT ARRESTED

The days that followed were a blur for Crox. He attended Pastor Carrie Seal's funeral, feeling an intense, profound sense of loss for his friend. The sudden death raised many questions, but with no evidence of foul play, the authorities ruled it an accident. The feeling that something darker was in the playwright's mind.

As the weeks passed, the investigation into Sherry's death hit a dead end, and there were no new leads on the suspected killer and cat shooter, Sean Palmer. Relda had her hands full with this and other cases, and He had not heard from her since PastorSeal's funeral.

Crox felt a growing sense of frustration and helplessness.

The loss of Pastor Carrie Seal and the lack of progress in the investigation frustrated him, but there was very little he could do at the moment. He knew he would not be able to rely on the authorities alone to solve the mysteries surrounding Carrie's death, the Circle of the Eternal Shadow, or his mother's missing book.

Crox decided to take matters into his own hands and delved deeper into the occult world. He spent hours on the internet researching occult books and witchcraft practices. Crox also sought out experts and practitioners of the supernatural, hoping to find someone who could provide insight into the Circle of Eternal Shadow's activities.

One of his searches led him to a man named Jim Christ. After weeks of attempts to contact him by email and telephone, Crox was finally able to reach Mr. Christ by phone. Mr. Christ identified himself as a former priest who had moved away from the church many years ago. He had since become a private investigator, specializing in finding missing people who may have joined a cult.

When Crox asked Jim Christ about the Circle of the Eternal Shadow, Christ immediately changed the subject. Crox suggested they meet in person, and Jim Christ advised he would be available later that day. Mr. Christ lived just south of Fredericksburg, in Ashland, Virginia.

Crox set off to visit Jim Christ with Jax in the back seat. The home was located off a remote country back road, surrounded by a vast green forest. Crox went up a long drive, parking in front of the small yellow single-story house. He rang the doorbell, and a solemn-looking Jim Christ greeted him and had him sit on the sofa; the old man took his seat in an oversized wooden rocking chair.

Jim Christ was a small, thin man about sixty years old. Though small, he had a strength you could almost feel. He assumed this was not a man to underestimate. Crox told Jim Christ everything that had happened in the past few weeks and showed him the occult symbol on the pendant Sun-Moon had given him. Jim's eyes widened at the symbol, and he informed Crox that the Circle of the Eternal Shadow was a cult focused on worshiping a forest Shadow God. He revealed that the cult was led by three powerful witches who possessed the ability to steal souls, enslave spirits, and control weak minds. Crox had heard most of this before, but three witches? That was a first.

Crox asked, "Do you know who these three witches are?"

"Not all of them. I only know one, Analee Morgan, but another person may have taken her place when she left town."

"You know Analee Morgan?" Crox asked

"No, I do not know her personally. However, I realized she was one of the three when her daughter Starleena went missing. I had worked with the police during the original search for Starleena." Jim advised.

"How did you figure she was one of the three witches? Crox inquired.

It's just simple detective work. The Circle of Eternal Shadows has always been attached to the woods around Ramouth Church Road; it is their holy place, and Jaxson Diamond and Analee's property is located near the area. I am sure everyone who lives on that property is part of the Circle of the Eternal Shadow." Jim answered.

"I need to find Analee. I am sure she knows more about her daughter's disappearance than what she told the police. Can you help me locate her?" Crox requested.

"I'll look into finding Analee Morgan if you wish to hire me. I charge $1500 and all expenses." Jim Christ stated

Crox agreed to the terms. Jim said he would call if he found anything or the trail had gone dead.

Meanwhile, Relda was carrying out her investigation. She convinced her supervisor that Sean Palmer was a prime suspect in the death of Sherry Shew and was determined to make an arrest. She also believed that Sun-Moon was an accomplice and may be hiding the suspect, so she was able to get a warrant to search her home and business.

The following day, Relda and fellow members of the sheriff's Department raided the Galinda the Good Witch store, which also included Sun-Moons' living quarters above the stop. Hiding in a cellar deep below the building, Relda found the suspected killer and cat shooter, Sean Palmer. He was quickly handcuffed and taken away, along with his accomplice, Sun-Moon.

While Sean and Sun-Moon were booked in the Rappahannock Regional Jail, Crox traveled with Jax to the Commune. He parked his truck on the side of the road a short distance away on Ramouth Church Road, not wanting to raise suspicion from the property's inhabitants.

Crox knew confronting the residents alone could be risky, but Crox was willing to take that chance to find the answers to the questions spinning in his head. With Jax by his side, He approached the Commune quietly. He realized the place was utterly deserted.

No one was around, and all the homes on the property seemed empty. Crox went to Jacob's trailer, which was also vacant. Not a single piece of furniture was left in the place. It was clear everyone had moved out. The place was abandoned.

Crox went up to the only stick-built house on the property, as all the other homes were trailers, and was about to climb the steps to the door when a calico cat jumped out of the front window, hissing at him, its body puffing up in attack mode. Crox grabbed a nearby broom and chased the cat away. Upon entering the vacant house, he was met with the smell of incense and candles burning.

In the middle of the living room stood a makeshift altar. Photos of Sean Palmer, Sherry Shew, Carrie Seal, and Sun-Moon lay on it. A painting of his mother and himself as a young child, along with Jaxson Diamond, was hanging on a wall beside the altar. His heart sank as he looked at the painting. What was his connection to this place and the people involved in this cult? Crox felt mixed emotions—anger, fear, and longing for answers. He knew he had to learn more about the Circle of the Eternal Shadow and their plans, but the abandoned Commune provided no immediate help.

He walked outside, looking around the property, unsure what to do next. He looked down at Jax and said, "Well, what now?"

Jax looked up at him and winked, then walked toward the woods. Crox followed the cat, who turned back to ensure that Crox remained with him.

Jax stopped at a large tree and started clawing at it frantically. Crox looked puzzled and stood there when he heard Jax say, "*Here, look Here.*"

Crox bent down and started looking around the trunk of the tree. There was a hole in the back of it, and there was a black plastic bag. He pulled out the bag, sat down, and opened it up. In his hand lay the book *Death is the Beginning*, his mother's supposed spell book. Crox was in disbelief. He had found the book! He hugged Jax and then looked up at the sky. A small prayer escaped his lips.

All he wanted to do was sit down and read his mother's book. However, he knew he should not linger in the woods for long. Crox carefully tucked the book back into the bag and patted Jaxon on the head and said, "Thank you, my friend,"

Crox and Jax made their way back to his truck. He had to leave the Commune behind and find a safe place to examine the book's contents. Driving back home, he again felt that he was being watched, and the shadows around him seemed to move strangely as if they were alive. Once back at home, locked safely inside with Jax. Crox opened the book to read his mother's grimoire.

Diving into the pages, Crox found references to the three witches and their dark rituals. The book described the process of soul stealing and the creation of a powerful being called the Shadow, the keeper of souls. He shuddered at his mother's words. As Crox continued reading, he realized that the book contained dark magick and information on countering the witches' spells. He found one page that contained the spell to vanquish the Shadow to some other realm.

The only person who could cast the spell was someone who had escaped the Shadow's grasp. The page also showed a protection amulet, a drawing of a cat outline with horns—the same charm Sun-Moon had given him. He decided to take the book to Crox Home Sales Inc. and lock it up in his office.

Relda was interrogating Sun Moon and Sean Palmer at the sheriff's office. Sean held his tongue and had not said even one word since his capture. Sun Moon advised Relda that she and Sean were innocent, that Sean came to her for help, as someone was after him, and that he had not killed anyone. Relda listened intently but didn't let her guard down.

Relda knew that cult members could be persuasive and manipulative. She needed concrete evidence. She took the two suspects back to their jail cells and headed home. While getting in her car, Vonda appeared next to the vehicle.

"What are you doing here?" Relda asked

Vonda replied, "Sean is innocent, Relda. The true killer can't be arrested, and to bring peace to those who have died, we are going to need Sean and Sun-Moon."

"What are you smoking, woman? How do you know these two suspects?" Relda asked, frustration evident in her voice. "I want to find Sherry's killer and bring her justice. All the evidence so far points to Sean Palmer, and Sun-Moon may also be involved."

"I know it's hard to accept, but there are forces at play here that you can't comprehend. The Circle of the Eternal Shadow has been manipulating events, and these people are more dangerous than you can imagine. I know you have heard of the Circle; Crox is more connected to them than you know. He has been keeping things from you." Vonda stated.

Relda replied, "Why don't we call him and sit down and talk."

"I don't think Crox will sit down with me right now, so you are going to have to talk to him and convince him to come to me and bring me his mother's book," Vonda said.

"What are you talking about?" Relda asked.

"He will Know," Vonda said, then turned and walked away.

Relda yelled, "Woman, Have you lost your mind?"

Relda got in her car, tired and frustrated. All she wanted was to go home and take a bubble bath, but now she was headed to Crox's place. That man had some explaining to do.

As Relda drove, her mind raced with questions and doubts. Vonda's cryptic words had only added to her confusion.

She had known and trusted Crox for a long time, but there seemed to be more to his involvement in this case than he had let on. When she arrived at his house, she found him sitting in his office, surrounded by papers and books. He looked up as she entered, his expression a mix of surprise and concern.

"Relda, what brings you here?" Crox asked.

"I need some answers," Relda replied firmly. "Vonda just dropped a bombshell on me. She said there's more to this case and your connection to it than I know. What's going on?

Crox took a deep breath and decided it was time to trust and be open with Relda. He explained everything, from finding the book and knife at the Commune to the strange occurrences that had followed him since then. He also told her about the pendant Sun-Moon had given him and how it seemed to play a significant role with this Shadow, the cult seemed to worship. Crox shared his suspicions about the three cult witches and how Vonda had approached him at his mother's grave and was seeking the book; she had to be a part of the Circle of the Eternal Shadow.

Relda listened attentively, her expression shifting from skepticism to concern. Crox was clearly struggling internally, and she could sense the fear in his voice. As he recounted his experiences, she put her hand on his shoulder and said, "I'm sorry. You don't have to carry this burden alone, Crox. I wish you had come to me sooner with the whole story."

"I wasn't sure I could trust you either since you and Vonda used to be in a relationship but are still friends," Crox confessed.

Relda stated, "I don't know if I trust Vonda either. I'm your friend and a professional. I won't let my personal feelings for Vonda interfere with us getting to the bottom of what's going on and stopping any more deaths or disappearances.

Chapter 11

Another Mess

The dream started the same way it had many times before. Crox found himself in a grassy meadow under a giant oak tree. His cousin Danny was there. Sitting under the tree with his cousin, he felt safe and at peace.

The area was bathed in the warm glow of the setting sun, and the air was filled with the sweet scent of wildflowers. He and Danny discussed old times, reminiscing about their childhood adventures and family. They laughed and talked as if they were catching up after a long absence.

In his dream state, Crox mustered the courage to ask Danny about the secrets surrounding his mother and the Circle of the Eternal Shadow. Danny turned serious and looked into Crox's eyes with a knowing gaze. "Cuz, there's a lot you need to know, but I can't tell you everything. Some things you have to discover on your own,"

"But I need guidance, Danny," Crox pleaded. I'm lost and don't know where to turn or who I can trust."

"Trust in yourself. Your intuition will be your guide. You're not alone. You have friends who care about you. Just remember that there are dark forces at play. Stay alert."

He nodded, taking in Danny's words. "I miss you so much, Danny," he said, his voice choked with emotion.

"I miss you too, Cuz, but you need to let go of the past, focus on the present, and see your destiny through. The answers are within you, and the book your mother left behind holds the answers. Trust your instincts."

As the dream started to fade, Crox felt comforted. He woke up to find Jake sitting by his side.

Jax told him, "*It was time to use the book and find Analee. Starleena is dead and trapped. Analee can help free her.*"

"I don't know where to start," Crox stated.

"*Sun-Moon knows,*" Jax stated and then walked away.

Crox called the Sheriff's Department and asked to see Sun-Moon. Relda agreed, but only if she was there.

Along with Jax, he went to the police station where Sun-Moon was being held. She agreed to meet with him and Relda in the interrogation room. Sun-Moon told them that Analee was one of the three witches of the Circle of the Eternal Shadow.

"Are you one?' Relda asked

"No, I only knew two of the group's leaders, Analee and Jaxson; I never found out who the third was."

"How do you know this?" asked Crox

"Many members of the Circle shopped in my store. Most had no power and were just followers. However, I could feel the power of Analee and Jaxson."

Relda interrupted, "How do Sean Palmer and Sherry Shew fit in?"

"Sean was trying to stop the Shadow. Little Sherry was in the wrong place at the wrong time."Moon-Sun advised

"How so?" asked Crox

Sun-Moon responded, "Sherry had run away from home and had been living under the FalmouthBridge.

One night, while she was at Sammy T's, a restaurant near my shop on Caroline Street, Sherry stole Sean's wallet and took his credit card, which is why she had it when you found her body. Sean had nothing to do with her death."

"Do you know who killed that little girl?" Relda said in frustration.

"No one. Sherry may have slipped on the rocks by the river and fallen in." Sun-Moon answered.

"Why did he break into my house and shoot my cat?" Crox asked.

Sun-Moon looked at him darkly, "Why not ask the cat?"

"You Know about Jax?" Crox responded while looking down at the cat.

Before Sun-Moon Could respond, Jax hissed loudly, ran up, and clawed Sun-Moon's leg.

Relda yelled, "Get that damn animal out of here."Crox picked up Jax and took him to his truck.

"Well, you just screwed the pooch, little one," Crox told Jax as he shut the truck's door.

After the cat attack, Sun-Moon ended the meeting and requested to return to her cell.

"What now?" Crox Asked Relda

"I'm not sure since Sean Palmer is still refusing to talk. We are waiting for the autopsy report to determine the cause of death on Sherry."

Crox bid Relda farewell and headed back home. He planned to look through the *Death is the Beginning* spell-book.

On the drive, he tried to get information from Jax about what Sun-Moon had said. The cat just lay there with an air of agitation.

When Crox walked through the front door of his house, he was hit with a site of utter destruction. It appeared as if a tornado had run through every room of his home. No piece of furniture stood upright; every picture was torn off the wall, and holes were punched in the walls.

His first thought was to get out and call the police, but as his nerves settled down, Crox sensed no one was in the house. He started walking slowly through each room. As far as he could tell, nothing looked like it had been stolen.

His electronics, jewelry, and even the hundred dollars he had on his bedside table were there.

Whatever the intruder was looking for, they did not find it. He felt he knew what it was: his mother's grimoire. Crox walked out the front door, Jax right on his tail. "Oh no, you don't," he told Jax. We need some time apart if you don't tell me what you know."

Crox left Jax standing in the driveway as he raced to Crox Home Sales Inc.

When he arrived at his office, his heart started racing when he saw two Sheriff's cars in the parking lot. He ran in, and there in the lobby were three Sheriff deputies: Armand, the office manager, and Rochelle, one of the real estate agents who worked at the company.

"What happened?" He asked.

Armand spoke up: "Rochelle was alone working on a contract when she heard someone trying to break in the back door. She called the police and then me."

"Are you Okay, Rochelle?" He asked.

Rochelle responded, "Oh yeah, I have my .22 pistol and was about to put a cap in an ass if they got through the door."

"Did you see what they looked like?" Crox asked.

"I couldn't make out their features. They were wearing dark clothes and a hoodie. I couldn't even tell if it was a man or a woman. The police said they were patrolling the neighborhood. They dusted for fingerprints but did not find any." Rochelle stated and advised she was going home, that it was all a bit much, and that she would be working from home for a while. Crox completely understood.

Crox entered his private office and glanced around, relieved to see that the book was untouched and still in his safe. Sitting down at his desk, he opened *Death is the Beginning*. This book linked his mother's secrets and the Circle of the Eternal Shadow. It was now his, and somebody wanted it desperately. He knew that it held answers, but he also realized that those answers might unravel his reality further.

Taking a deep breath, he opened the book. His mother's handwriting, symbols, and diagrams filled its pages. It was a mix of personal anecdotes, spells, and a personal journal. He had read through it briefly when he first found it, but this time, he focused on the sections that might give him insight into Analee, Jaxson, and the third witch who controlled the cult.

Crox stumbled upon a passage that made his heart race. It spoke of a hidden sanctuary where the Circle of the Eternal Shadow performed their most secretive rituals. The description hinted at an underground cavern located deep within the forest, concealed and protected by magick. He realized, based on the description his mother laid out in the book, that it was the same area where he had his accident all those years ago. The same place where he found both Lucky and Jax. If this area was supposed to be hidden, why had he stumbled upon it twice?

Crox could no longer ignore the coincidences—he had encountered this hidden area twice in his life. There had to be a reason fate had brought him to this place, and the answers he sought seemed to lie within the depths of that underground cavern. Crox stood from his desk and grabbed his car keys and the book. He would find out what was hidden beneath the forest of Ramouth Church Road.

When Crox was about to leave, Armand stopped him to see if he had any instructions. Crox said, "No, just keep down the fort and let me know if anything that needs my attention comes up.".

Armand asked, "What is that? That's a strange-looking book. Can I see it?" Crox ignored the questions and said, "I'll be out of the office for a few days. Call me if you need me." Armand looked annoyed as he watched Crox walk out the door.

The anticipation and uncertainty of what lay ahead weighed heavily on his mind as he drove towards Ramouth Church Road and back to the forest. The spell book sat on the passenger seat, a constant reminder of the possible danger he could be in. Crox wondered if he could be walking into a trap and if the same person or persons who had ransacked his home were now leading him on somehow.

Crox turned off Route One onto Ramouth Church Road. The truck seemed to know where it was going on its own. Approaching the area near where he had his accident years ago, he noticed his tire imprints were still in the dirt from the night he and Relda had been there. He also noticed another set of tire imprints. Someone else had been there not long ago. The surroundings seemed to grow darker, though it was still daylight. The trees seemed to close in on the road, casting long shadows that danced eerily in the fading light.

Crox's heart raced, his grip on the steering wheel tightening with each passing moment. Crox glanced at the book, its pages glowing slightly in the twilight. He took a deep breath and reached for the book. It was time to go to the area outlined by his mother. The book described a specific path to follow, a set of landmarks that would guide him to the entrance of the underground cavern.

Feeling he could find it easily, Crox armed himself with a flashlight and the book. He began walking through the trees. The forest was alive with the sound of rustling leaves and the occasional snap of a twig underfoot. There was also the sound of howling coming from within the woods. Anxiety and fear washed over him as he followed the path, his flashlight cutting through the darkness. The symbols and descriptions in the book matched the environment around him, confirming he was on the right track.

After what felt like an eternity of navigating the dense woods, he came upon the circle of rocks, and the large pentagram burned into the ground. He was back. As he entered the center of the rocks, the ground beneath his feet trembled slightly under him. An invisible entrance seemed to materialize. The opening was narrow, just wide enough for him to squeeze through. As he was about to go through the entrance to the cavern, he heard a voice behind him.

"Don't goin there. If you do, you won't come out alive." He turned to see Vonda walking toward him from behind a tree.

Vonda's presence was unexpected and sent a wave of anger through him. Her eyes bore into him with a mix of concern and urgency.

"Vonda, what the hell are you doing here?" He asked, his voice betraying both surprise and suspicion.

Vonda's expression remained serious, and her lips pressed into a thin line. "You're walking into something far more dangerous than you can imagine. If you go further, the Shadow will finally have you. Give me that book, and get out of here."

"Who do you think you are, and why in the fuck would I give you this book?" Crox cried out, then continued, "You are the one who broke into my house, aren't you?"

"I'm trying to protect you. You have to believe me," Vonda pleaded

"Protect me? how?" Crox asked in frustration

"Your mother had planned to sacrifice you to the Shadow to circumvent her leadership in the Circle of the Eternal Shadow. She did not like the fact that three witches controlled the Shadow and ruled the group together. Pittapat wanted her power as high priestess to control the group, including the other two, Jaxson and Analee, her son and his girlfriend."

Crox looked confused. "Why would she want to give me to this Shadow thing? I am also her son."

"The Shadow asked for your life since you escaped it. When you had your accident in this forest, the Shadow came for your soul. It always gets the souls that come into the forest. However, you were saved. You got away from its grasp, and the Shadow never forgot."

"Well, Damn." was the only response Crox could make.

Vonda continued her story, " I was a Circle of the Eternal Shadow member. Our true goal was to keep the Shadow contained in the forest. Pittapat, though, wanted to use its power for her own plans. When I found out what she would do to you, I left the group and befriended you to watch over you. Please believe me. I love you and want to keep you safe, but as long as you have that book and come here, you are taking risks with your life."

"Who else is involved with the Circle of the Eternal Shadow? Crox asked.

"There are many. I do not know all the members. Since Jaxson died and Analeed disappeared, I do not know who is now in charge of the group." Vonda Responded

Crox was in disbelief and felt a sense of betrayal. Vonda's story was jarring, and he struggled to process the information she had just revealed. He gazed at her, gauging if she was telling the truth. "You expect me just to hand over this book and trust you? How can I know you're not just trying to manipulate me?"

Vonda's expression softened, and she took a step closer."I understand your skepticism, but please, you have to believe me. I care about you, and I want to keep you safe. The power within that book is beyond your comprehension and could attract all sorts of dark things."

"What do you suggest I do then?" Crox asked, his voice cracking as he tried to hold back tears.

"Destroy the book, and let the past remain buried," Vonda urged. "You have people who care about you and want to see you live a normal, safe life. Let's leave this darkness behind us and move forward."

"Give me some time to think about all this," Crox said, his voice heavy with uncertainty. I need to figure out what to do next."

Vonda nodded understandingly. "Take your time. Just remember that your safety is my priority. I will be here if you need me."With that, Vonda turned and disappeared into the forest's darkness, leaving Crox standing there, feeling the anger take hold of him again.

Chapter 12

EVERYONE CONNECTED?

Crox made his way home. As he drove, he thought of all that had happened. Funny, barely a month ago, he was living an everyday, monotonous life, work, friends, and everyday drums. Now he was tangled in what? He did not know. He had a cat in his house that talked when it wanted to, and he had a cult possibly after him, not to mention a shadowy creature.

Also, his mother might have tried to kill him. Crox was determined to get information from Jax and, hopefully, find out what happened to Starleena. In his heart, he knew she was dead. One thing was: sure, Jax had information regarding the forest and its inhabitants.

When Crox arrived home, he parked his truck and sat staring at the house, letting out a deep sigh, wishing for normalcy in his life. The house was still in disarray from the break-in. Jax was waiting for him in the driveway, perched on the front porch railing.

He approached Jax slowly, his mind racing. "Alright, Jax, we need to talk. I need answers, and I need them now."

Jax looked up at him, his eyes conveying a mixture of annoyance and resignation. "*You are just like your mother. Fine, I suppose it's time to reveal a bit more information.*"

Crox sat down in the driveway, looking intently at Jax. "First of all, how can you communicate with me like this? He asked.

"*I can talk to you because I can traverse the worlds of the living and the dead. I have been able to see ghosts since I was human. A powerful witch taught me how to open myself to the other realm." Jax responded*

Crox's eyes widened in realization. " The Circle of the Eternal Shadow, it was all starting to make sense. He did find Jax at the place where the cult kept their little secret, the Shadow.

"Are you a part of the Circle of the Eternal Shadow?"

No response.

"Jax, Answer me!" Crox cried out.

Jax responded, "The real question you should be asking is, where is Analee? That, my dear sir, is what I am here to do: help you find her."

"Alright, let's find Analee," Crox stated.

The cat seemed satisfied as he ran off to the back porch. The phone rang, it was Jim Christ. "Hello, Crox. I wanted to call and let you know I found Analee Morgan and where she is staying."

"That is great; where can I find her?" Crox asked.

"I followed her to the Village of Idlewild. She is staying at 111 Augustine Drive." Jim answered.

"Thanks for the information. I will mail a check for your services. " Crox realized Analee's address belonged to his office manager, Armand. This was getting weirder. He called Relda and told her about Jim Christ's find. Relda suggested getting Armand away from his house, and she said she would go check out his place. She couldn't get inside without a warrant or probable cause of a crime, but she could at least walk around the house and look in the windows.

Crox called Armand at Crox Home Sales Inc., who was still at the office. "Hey, Armand, I must talk to you about a few things. It's important. Can we meet?"

Armand stated he had a lot of work to do. Crox suggested a quick lunch and a drink break, and Armand agreed since he was his boss.

He suggested meeting at Cowboy Jack's, a restaurant near the Village of Idlewild, where Armand lived.

Crox arrived a little early, grabbing a seat by the window so he could see Armand coming. He would text Relda when he saw him pull into the parking lot. She was waiting around the block from Armand's house. When Relda was sure Armand was being contained, she would search around his house and see if anyone was there.

Thirty minutes passed, and Armand was nowhere to be seen. Then, just when he was about to give up, he saw Armand's vehicle turn in the parking lot.

Crox texted Relda to keep an eye out. He would try to keep Armandat at the restaurant as long as possible.

The two men talked for a while about the real estate brokerage. Crox looked to see any nervousness in Armand's tone or manner. The man was cool as a cucumber.

He came out and asked Armand if he knew Analee Morgan. Armand became defensive and deflected the question. Instead of answering, Armand asked his own: "How do you know Analee?"

I don't. She is a missing person as well as a possible suspect in her daughter's disappearance," Crox stated bluntly.

Armand's eyes widened slightly, and he shifted uncomfortably in his seat before responding. "I have heard of her but don't know her personally. Why would she be a suspect in her own daughter's disappearance?"

"Stop lying! I have it on good authority that you know her and may hide her at your home," Crox shouted. Thankfully, the restaurant wasn't busy, so only a few people at the bar turned in their direction.

Armand Stood up stated, "I think this conversation is over; I'm leaving."

"You do, and not only will you be fired, but you may also get arrested as an accomplice. Starleena's disappearance is still an active case."

Armand huffed under his breath and sat back down.

"Well, answer me; how do you know Analee."

"My personal life is none of your business. It has nothing to do with my job."

He was hitting a wall. Armand was not going to talk. He was about to get more forceful, but his phone vibrated just as he was about to press further.

Crox received a text from Relda. He discreetly checked the message under the table. Relda's message read, "Armand's place is clear. There are no signs of anyone else there, but there is a lot of weirdness going on in the house. Let's meet back at your place."

Crox stood up and said, "This isn't over. We will talk again soon, and I expect answers." With that, he left the restaurant, leaving Armand with the bill.

He made his way home. Jax was sitting on the porch, patiently waiting. As he walked into the house, he felt Jax say in his mind, *Still pissy?* This caught him off guard, causing him to burst out laughing.

He knew he was involved even though he got nothing out of Armand. Finding Analee was just a matter of time. Since she was one of the supposed witches in the Circle of Eternal Shadows, perhaps she could shed more light on the Shadow, Starleena, and his mother's book.

Crox smiled and said to himself, "Well, Ms. Analee, to quote Ricky Ricardo. You got sum'splaining to do, Lucy."

Not long after he did, Relda showed up. She walked in without knocking and asked, "Who the hell do you have working for you?"

He was taken aback. "Armand has been with the company for over five years; I have never had a problem with him." It was true; Armand had been a model agent and doing a fantastic job running the real estate firm since he became the supervisor.

Relda explained that when she got to Armand's house, all the shades were drawn in front of it. She went up and knocked on the door, but there was no answer. She stated she stood there and listened at the door but didn't hear anything.

She went around the house, knocked, and listened at the back door, but there was no movement. As she was leaving, she noticed no curtain in the kitchen window. Relda went on to describe what she saw.

The kitchen was painted deep red. In the middle of the floor was a pentagram with what looked like a cat's head in the middle of the pentagram. A large pot was cooking on the stove; I couldn't see what was in it.

"I've called the district judge to get a search warrant. I can at least get him for animal cruelty, but something else is going on in that house."

He didn't know what to say. He had never been to Armand'shouse. He never had a reason to visit him. It then dawned on him. Armand must be a part of the Circle of the Eternal Shadow. It was becoming increasingly clear that this cult had infiltrated various aspects of his life. But why? Was everyone in his life connected?

As Relda spoke, Jax sat beside him, taking it all in intently. Starleena's ghost was also there. She told Jax, "You must get them all to the forest. With their help, my mom will save me and the others from our entrapment." Jax understood and knew exactly how he would return them to the forest. He was going to have to come clean and tell him the truth.

Relda stated there was not much more they could do until the search warrant arrived. Also, Relda wanted to let him know some troubling news. Sherry Shew's autopsy came back, and even though her death appeared to be suspicious, the coroner ruled the death accidental.

The D.A. was not going to charge Sean Palmer with the girl's murder. The only thing the Sheriff's office had on him was the breaking into his house and the discharge of a firearm in the commission of a crime. Relda advised Sean Palmer could post bond and get out of jail.

Relda advised that the D.A. also decided not to charge Sun-Moon with aiding and abetting a fugitive. She was released that morning.

"I don't think I have anything to worry about from Sun-Moon, but what do you think about Sean Palmer? Do you think he'll come back here?" asked Crox, who leaned back in his chair, running a hand through his hair in frustration.

"I've got officers keeping an eye on your property just in case he decides to pay another visit.

I would also suggest you keep your Smith and Wesson on you and ensure all the doors and windows are locked."

He sighed heavily, looking at Jax. "I know. We're going to have to be careful and watch our backs." Jax nodded and meowed in agreement.

"That being said, we all need some time to recharge. I'm going to go home and take a nap," crooned Rodella as she stood up to leave. "Let me know if you need anything."

He watched as Relda pulled out of the driveway, feeling exhaustion overtake him. The past few weeks' events had taken a toll on him physically and emotionally. He glanced over at Jax, who was still sitting on the couch. He focused on something in the corner that he could not see.

What he could not see in the empty spot in the corner was Starleena looking in his direction with a mischievous smile. She looked at Jax and said, "It's time to tell him everything."

It was time for him to return to the Forest and face the Shadow. He needed to end what his mother had controlled. It was time for him to fulfill the destiny fate had laid out for him soon.

Jax turned to face Crox and asked. "*Are you ready to hear the whole story and face your family's demons?*"

Crox was unsure if he was ready. However, he now had no choice but to hear the cat out. But first, he needed to clear his mind and rest his body.

Crox stepped into the steamy embrace of the hot shower, feeling the water cascade over his skin like a soothing baptism. The warm droplets danced gently across his body, washing away the grime and tension of the day.

As he stood under the stream, he couldn't help but reflect on his current state—lost, confused, and in desperate need of salvation. Little did he know that the life he thought he was living was nothing more than a false reality, a mere waking dream that would soon be shattered by the harsh truth awaiting him.

Chapter 13

Jax's Story

Crox stepped out onto his back deck, fresh from a warm shower. In one hand, he held a crystal tumbler filled with bourbon and in the other, a thick cigar. The cool night air nipped at his damp skin, sending shivers down his spine.

Earlier in the evening, when Relda had left, Crox secured every lock on the house and carefully drew all the curtains closed. With Sean Palmer released on bond that morning and free to roam the town, Crox couldn't help but feel a sense of unease. Would Sean attempt to break into the house again? The reason for his previous break-in and shooting of Jax still remained a mystery. Even the cat who witnessed it all was tight-lipped about the incident.

Crox couldn't shake off the feeling of unease as he took another sip of his drink and gazed into the night sky.

While Crox enjoyed his bourbon and cigar, letting his mind wander, Jax jumped up on the chair beside him. The cat's black fur glistened in the moonlight, and his emerald green eyes reflected the evening stars. He was indeed a beautiful creature.

Jax sat staring at him, finally getting the courage to speak to him telepathically.

"I have much to tell you. There is a reason you came back to the woods the night you found me. You were drawn back to the forest of Ramouth Church Road. The Shadow called you to come. I was there waiting for you to come back."

"Go on, I'm listening," Crox said as he sat back with his hands crossed over his chest.

Jax's Story:

"I am not a typical cat, which I am sure you have figured out. I was not always in the form of a cat. I was a human man in my previous life before I was killed. This form is the reincarnation of my spirit after escaping the Shadow that trapped my soul.

My name in the human world was Jaxson Diamond. I am your brother. Like our mother, I was a witch. My girlfriend Analee is also a witch. The three of us became the keepers of the Shadow. The Circle of the Eternal Shadow was created to keep the Shadow in the forest.

Our bloodline is not connected to the witch Victoria Parham, who called forth the Shadow, but our magic is connected thanks to the book Death is the Beginning. *Our mother brought together all the spells and rituals belonging to the past witches who had controlled the Shadow over the last hundred years and created one powerful book.*

Most Circle of the Eternal Shadow members are low-level practitioners of witchcraft; they are primarily followers whose families shun them.

Although most do not have much power over the Shadow, they are loyal and serve other purposes within the group.

Unfortunately, we must sacrifice a group member to keep the Shadow contained. The shadow needed souls to keep it happy. All those who were sacrificed did so of their own free will. We had to do this to keep the Shadow contained in the forest. Sometimes, some unlucky person would enter the forest and be taken by the Shadow. We tried to prevent this whenever possible, which is one of the reasons I bought the property. We tried to keep people from trespassing.

You do not remember me and why there was a rift between you and our mother. It all started when you had your accident. You see, our aunt Maryann was also a member of the Circle of Eternal Shadows, along with her son Danny, our cousin. She was supposed to watch over you and keep you safe whenever you visited the area. Mother knew Danny died in the forest at the hands of the Shadow. His soul was trapped, and Mother was afraid for you and placed watchers to protect you.

On the night of your accident, you had been visiting Aunt Maryann, and after you left, you wrecked your car near the woods where the Shadow dwells. Maryann should not have allowed you to visit her at night when the Shadow's powers are strongest. That is why Mother sacrificed her to the Shadow not long after she learned of the accident. Our mother was a vengeful woman.

While you were trapped in the wreckage, the Shadow came to take your soul, but you were saved. A tiny grey and white kitten with the same green eyes that I have was saved. That kitten was the embodiment of Danny. If a soul can escape the Shadow's grasp, it comes back into this realm as a cat.

The Shadow lost and was unable to trap your soul, thanks to Danny saving you.

Did you ever wonder why Lucky lived so long? Cats have an average life span of twelve to fifteen years, but Lucky was twenty-eight years old. He used his little power to protect you for as long as he could. We are spirits coming back into this realm, no matter what form. We still have whatever powers we had as humans, but they are not as strong.

When Mother learned what had happened, she went mad. She killed her sister for not protecting you. She then had Analee and me help her do a spell to erase your memory of the Shadow, Analee, and me. Our mother did not want you around the Circle of the Eternal Shadow coven or anyone who practiced witchcraft, hoping you would never come back to the forest.

When the spell was complete, you had no memory of me or the commune. The fight you had with our mother, well, that was real; you two were always like oil and water. Lucky was there to watch over you and ensure you never returned to Ramouth Church Road.

The Shadow became harder to control after that. No one had ever escaped it before, and it became enraged at the loss of your soul. Our mother also started diving deeper and deeper into the black arts, looking for ways to control the evil of the forest. She became obsessed with black magic and was overtaken by its power.

Analee and I tried to reason with her, but it became impossible when she made a deal with the Shadow. She said that with its power, she could control it even more. It was all lies; there was no true way to control that evil creature fully.

The Shadow manipulated our mother, tempting her with promises of power to lure you to it. It convinced Mother to deliver you so it could use your powers for its own gain.

Analee and I saw through its deceit; we knew the truth - that it had no intention of sparing your life once you were within its grasp.

That is why I have been watching you all these years, following you around, trying to find ways to give you hints about our mother without breaking the spell. The Circle members also saw the evil changes in Pittapat, and together, we agreed to send Vonda to get close to you. It was too risky for me to be in your life.

Mother died not long after the deal she made with the Shadow; I suspect it was at the hands of another one of our members, Sean Palmer. Sean knew what she was doing and told us he would not allow her to continue her power grab and sacrifice you. The two of you were a couple before we wiped your memory.

After our mother died, we lost control of the Shadow. The Shadow's power was stronger than I was aware of. It would call through space and time, inviting people in our bloodline to come to it in the forest. My daughter Starleena was the weakest and closest to the forest when it called out to her first.

The night Starleena was taken, Analee and I went to dinner in Fredericksburg. The Shadow had been quiet for some time, and we did not think it was active. Our ignorance cost us our daughter's life. Had we known, we would have never left the property. We didn't think she had gone to Ramouth Church Road for some time. Weeks went by, and she was nowhere to be found. The police and the members of the Circle of EternalShadows could not locate her. We had no idea what could have happened to her; Analee and I were a wreck.

One night, as I was about to fall asleep, I heard the siren of the Shadow. It called to me, though I was unsure what it was then. It was just a voice in my head. It called for me to come to the circle in the forest, where the witches worked the spell that controlled the Shadow.

Once in the forest, I realized the shadow had enticed me to come. I was a powerful witch, but I was not powerful enough alone to confront the Shadow. Before I had a chance to run, the Shadow killed me. Once dead, I was able to see Starleena. It was only for a second, and then the Shadow forced her back into the cavern, where it kept its trapped souls.

The Shadow offered me a deal. If I helped it capture you, it would allow my soul to cross back over to this realm. If I did not, it would trap my soul for eternity, feeding off its essence. I am sad to say I agreed, but only if the Shadow would release Starleena's soul and let her cross to the other side or return to this realm. I made a deal with the devil—my brother's life for my daughter's soul.

I'm sorry. I was crazed by the thought of Starleena's soul forever being trapped by that thing. Once the deal was struck, the Shadow released my soul. I came back, not as a human, but as the cat you see before you.

The form you see me in now is the form all souls who do not crossover but come back to this realm become. All cats are people who do not go into the light. I don't understand it myself. However, all souls trapped by the Shadow who either escape its clutches or are allowed to be released can keep their human memories.

Once the shadow released my soul, I waited for you in the forest to come. The Shadow called out to you, its song ringing in your mind until you returned to it. It took weeks, but you eventually succumbed to its calling.

When I saw you wandering through the woods, I knew you were under the Shadow's spell.

In the end, I couldn't let the Shadow have you. You are my brother, after all. You are also still under Pittapat's memory spell, so I knew you would not remember me. The spell can be broken, and I will help you to free Starleena together.

I need your help to stop the Shadow. I cannot do it alone. Together, we can free all the souls trapped in the cavern."

Crox sat there with his mouth open. What could he say? It was a lot to take in. He was in shock. Finally, his cigar fell out of his fingers onto his leg, causing him to jump up and spill his drink all over himself, bringing him out of his mind fog. He wiped the spilled bourbon off his pants and took a deep breath.

"So tell me this: If Sean and I were a couple, why did he break into my house and shoot you?" Crox asked.

"Sean was looking for your mother's book. He thinks he can use it to end your memory spell. He shot me because he still believes I am working with the Shadow." Jax responded.

"Are you?" Crox said with a touch of anger in his voice.

"No, I need you. You are the only one left in our bloodline. You can stop this nightmare."

Crox thought to himself how he longed to end both his living and sleeping nightmares.

With Sean Palmer now out of jail, he might be hard to track down, but then again, he might also be keeping close. Crox would need to trust Relda and fill her in. Hopefully, with her being Sheriff, she could track Sean down. Vonda might also have more information, which could be helpful, but could she be trusted?

Crox decided first to swing by his office and grab the book *Death is the Beginning* from his safe.

He would also have to change the locks because, at this point, Armand was no longer part of Crox Home Sales Inc. It was becoming increasingly frustrating that he could not trust anyone in his life. Armand and Vonda were both members of the Circle of the Eternal Shadow. Who else?

Unsure about Relda, Crox realized he had to trust someone. There was also Sun-Moon. She said she wasn't a member of the cult, but he was not 100 percent positive she was telling the truth.

Crox now knew Analee's hiding place and was determined to pay her a visit. He needed to hear her side of the story. Unsure whether or not he would bring Jax with him, he also wondered if he could trust this cat anymore.

Chapter 14

Call of the Shadow

After Jax finished his story, Crox decided to go to bed early. He knew tomorrow would be a busy day, and tonight, he needed to get some much-needed rest. He always knew his family was crazy, but this took the cray-cray to a whole new level.

Crox was not asleep long before the nightmare came. This dream started with him as a young boy. He was sitting on the floor at his mother's feet in an old single-wide trailer. She was reading to him from an old book—no, not reading, chanting. She was encouraging him to chant along. As time passed, Crox was no longer a young boy in the trailer but was now a grown man; he found himself in the forest where he had that fateful car crash.

Crox watched himself in the dream chanting. A sudden gust of wind whizzed by him, and he turned to see a beautiful woman with large breasts and child-bearing hips. Her long, silky dark hair went down to the middle of her back, and she had bright green eyes looking at him from a clearing in the woods. She extended a hand to him, and he hesitantly took it, feeling strangely drawn to her beauty.

The woman then revealed to him that she had been calling to him. She explained that he was also calling out to her with his chants. They were meant to be together. As she unrobed, she invited him to join her in a circle of rocks.

"My dear Crox, here is where you will find peace within my embrace. I can give you power that you could never dream was possible. I will make you more powerful than any witch before you. All I ask is that you give me your soul."

Crox awoke with a start, falling out of bed onto the floor. He got up and grabbed his phone; the time was 3:20 a.m. As he lay there, he heard a song in his head. Something was very familiar about its melody. He arose and started walking toward the front door. Jax leaped in front of his legs, causing him to trip and smash face-first onto the floor again.

"No," He heard in his mind. *"It's the call of the Shadow. Shake it off."*

The fall brought him to his senses. Crox still heard the song, but it was no longer as powerful.

"Well, I guess I'm not getting any more sleep tonight," Crox said out loud as he headed to the kitchen to make a pot of strong coffee. He knew he had to prepare himself. It was going to be a long day. After breakfast and some much-needed caffeine, Crox gathered up Jax and headed over to meet Relda at Crox HomeSales Inc.

Crox wanted to be on his home turf. While there, he would change the office locks and email the other agents, letting them know not to contact Armand or allow him in the office.

On the drive to the office, Crox began singing, realizing the song was the same one from his dream that he was chanting. He wasn't sure why he was doing it, but it strangely comforted him. He started feeling internally powerful. When he arrived at the real estate brokerage, he went straight to his office and changed the locks. He was furious with Armand. How could he have worked with this man all these years and not know he was a part of his mother's cult? He also realized he had missed that Vonda was also a part of it, and he had been closer to her.

Crox noticed that Jax had run off when they walked into the building. He looked around, but the cat was nowhere in sight. He called for Jax several times but got no response. He looked in the front reception area but did not find him there either. Then, he heard something. It was a strange faint sound coming from the back of the office. He followed the sound until it became louder and more precise. It had the same tone as the chant from his dream. Jax was staring out of a window. The cat turned. looked at him and telepathically said, "*The Shadow is growing stronger and more powerful. We need to come up with a plan soon.*"

"What is it, Jax? What's happening?" Crox whispered, anxiety evident in his voice.

Jax turned back the window, his eyes fixed on something only the feline could see.

Jax saw the vision of his daughter, Starleena. The Shadow used her to draw Crox and Jax back to the forest, where it would consume them both. The pain on Starleena's face was more than Jax could bear. He vowed to save his daughter's soul, no matter the price.

Relda got to the office at 11:00 a.m. She went over the scene at Armand's house again. She said a search warrant would be in momentarily and invited Crox to come along. The search warrant was only based on the potential animal cruelty charge, based on the cat head she saw in the middle of the pentagram through the window. Hopefully, they would be able to catch Armand off guard and find Analee, as well as any other criminal acts that would allow the Sheriff's Department to hold both Armand and Analee in jail for questioning.

They rode together in Relda's squad car, dropping Jax off on the front porch of Crox's house. He was not going to leave the cat inside the house alone anymore after he destroyed it last time, and he was also still unnerved by Jax's story. As they pulled up to Armand's house, Crox noticed someone pulling back the curtain in the front window.

"Well, I guess someone is home." Crox stated to Relda, who replied, "It's game time. Put on your ass-kicking boots."

They approached the door, and Relda knocked loudly, announcing it was the Sheriff's Department with a search warrant. There was no response. At this time, a backup Sheriff pulled up and went around back in case someone tried to leave by the back door. Relda continued knocking and, finally getting fed up, yelled," If you don't open this door now, I am breaking it down!"

An aggressive-looking, short, middle-aged Hispanic woman with cropped black hair answered the door. She looked at them and said, *No habla ingles*, which meant, "I don't speak English."Relda answered her back in Spanish, advising her that she spoke Spanish. The woman's face grew dark, and she looked at Relda with narrow eyes and said, "What the hell do you want, Cop?" All said in perfect English.

"My, you learned English quick, huh," Relda said sarcastically.

Relda presented the search warrant and asked for the woman's identification. She turned over her wallet; sure enough, it was Analee Morgan, Starleena Diamond's mother and possible witch of the Circle of the Eternal Shadow. Relda informed Analee she was under arrest for suspected animal cruelty and that they could have more charges once the search was completed.

Analee began protesting, but Relda quickly cut her off. She would answer all her questions at the station. She was then handcuffed and taken away in the squad car headed for lock up. They were free to enter the house and start their search. The air inside felt heavy and smelled of strong incense. Moving through the rooms, they saw various signs of occult practices: pentagrams etched on the kitchen floor, candles of different colors arranged in patterns, and strange symbols painted on the walls. The house was a bizarre mix of mundane beige decor and sinister dark mysticism.

Jars containing what seemed to be dried herbs and what looked like dried animal parts were scattered around multiple rooms. In a corner of an upstairs bedroom, a makeshift altar adorned with bones and feathers was set up. They discovered a hidden room behind a bookshelf in the basement. This room seemed to be where Analee had been staying. A bed and dresser with women's clothing. There was also another makeshift altar with pictures of Analee, Jaxson, and Starleena and photos of Pittapat and Crox.

Relda's s expression turned grim as she surveyed the scene. "Well, there are no animals here; these bones and the cat head in the kitchen are quite old. I don't have anything to hold Analee or Armand on. However, I want to question them both. I can hold them for at least 24 hours."

Relda advised some of the Sheriffs to continue searching and report back to her at the Sheriff's office. She then radioed to have Armand picked up once found and brought in.

"Let's see what we can get from Ms. Morgan. Come on," Relda stated to Crox.

While on the drive to the Sheriff's office, Crox's mind was abuzz with all the questions he wanted to ask Analee. He knew he would only have a short time to get information from her. He had to figure out how to get her to talk and not have her clam up. They arrived at the Sheriff's office with Analee Morgan in custody. She was placed in an interrogation room while Crox and Relda waited outside, going over their approach. Crox was determined to get answers, not only about Starleena and Sean Palmer but also about the Circle of the Eternal Shadow. He also wanted to compare her story with Jax's.

Relda leaned in and whispered to him, "Let me take the lead on this initially. I have dealt with a fair share of suspects and have a way of getting them to open up."

Crox nodded in agreement. He knew that her approach to a police officer might yield better results. They entered the interrogation room together, taking their respective seats across the table from Analee. Analee was sitting at a small conference table, her left hand shackled to the chair, which was bolted to the floor.

Relda began, her voice calm but firm: "Ms. Morgan, we have evidence that you've been involved in some questionable activities, including the disappearance of your daughter and potential connections to a cult. We want to understand your involvement and the extent of your association with the Circle of the Eternal Shadow."

Analee's eyes darted between them. Her initial defiance seemed to waver, and she hesitated before speaking. "Look, you don't understand. The Circle is not what you think. We're just an abiding religious organization."

Crox leaned forward, his voice edged with bitterness, "Really? That's not what Jax tells us; you know Jax, the cat who used to be a man named Jackson Diamond. Isn't he the father of your daughter Starleena?"

Analee sighed, her shoulders slumping slightly. "How much do you know?" she asked suspiciously.

"Enough to know that you are lying right now. I have a talking cat at my house who says he is my brother, and you were his girlfriend. Care to explain?"

With a knowing smile, Analee said, "You know more than I thought you did. Are you ready to fulfill your destiny and finish what Jaxson and I started?"

"And what is my destiny?" Crox asked.

"To send the Shadow back from where it came from and release the souls it has trapped, which includes my daughter, who is also your niece."

Relda jumped in, "So you know where Starleena is? Tell me what happened to your daughter and where we can find her."

Crox looked at Relda and back at Analee, saying simply, "We're listing. Tell us what you know."

Just then, an officer burst in and said they arrested Armand. He was currently being booked and getting his mugshot done. Relda advised them to put him in a holding cell. She would call for him when they were done with Analee.

The officer said Armand requested a call to his lawyer. Relda advised that it was his right to make the call. She also advised him to take notes of anything Armand said, no matter how strange it was.

Analee burst out laughing, "Strange... You don't know the half of it. Once you know the truth, your mortal minds may explode."

"I'm sure our little mortal minds can easily understand what you have to say, madam," Relda growled.

"Well, I guess you need to know the whole story and confirm what Jax told you. If you must know the full story, it will help us defeat the Shadow." Crox crossed his arms and said, "Well, go on then, tell us your story." Analee threw her head back and laughed. Under her breath, she said, "Boy, are you in for it now?"

Chapter 15

Analee's Tale

Analee asked for a strong cup of coffee and a Pall Mall cigarette. "I might as well smoke if I'm chained to this chair. How about you uncuff me, Sheriff?"

"Not a chance." Relda flatly stated. "Now tell us what you know."

Annalee's Story:

"I grew up in Cuba and came to the U.S. when I was twenty. My family spoke Spanish and English, so getting a job and starting a new life was easy when I moved to this country. I moved here to escape the prosecution of my small town. They were a small-minded and superstitious people.

I have known I was different from an early age. I could see the dead and communicate with spirits that had never been human. My family just ignored it for the most part, but I know it scared them.

When people in my town discovered I could see the dead, they accused me of being a witch—a bruja—*and ran me out of town. No one in my family stood up for me. I came to this country with the clothes on my back and the $300 I stole from my grandfather.*

After a few years in Florida, I made my way to Virginia and settled in Stafford County, where I met members of the Circle of the Eternal through Sun-Moon. Sun-Moon can see magical powers in others, which I guess is her power. After I joined the coven, I started to learn how to summon the dead at will and be able to control low-level spirits.

I did not meet Pittapat, the high priestess, until a year later. She came to me one night with her son Jaxson; she told me of the three witches, who were the group's leaders and in charge of keeping an evil entity contained.

She and Jaxson were two of the witches, along with her nephew Danny. Unfortunately, Danny had just died, and they needed someone with the power to call on spirits to take his place in the coven.

The power of the Witches' Three was based on blood, and since I was not a blood relative, she did a spell to bind Jaxson to me in a spiritual marriage. I had to conceive a child with him so our blood would be intertwined. Starleena was the result of that union. I was only to be a part of the Witches' Three until Starleena came of age and was powerful enough to call on spirits herself so she could take my place.

By this time, your mother had already put the memory spell on you; she did not want you to join the commune. She felt you had no power to call on spirits, and your safety would be at risk. I had never met you before now. Jaxson was devastated by what your mother had done. He never wanted you to be removed from the family or the coven.

Your partner, Sean Palmer, had always been suspicious of her. The two of them never got along, which is why she allowed his memory of you and your relationship. Sun-Moon, however, found a way to break the spell on him after her death.

While you were living your best life in Fredericksburg, Jaxson, your mother, and I were busy keeping the world safe from the Shadow. You had always been able to control your mother in a way that Jaxson couldn't, and with you no longer in her life, she started to lose control of her power and started practicing more dark arts.

As high priestess, she controlled the Circle of Eternal Shadows with an iron fist. She never listened to Jaxson or me, even though she needed our power to prevent the Shadow from escaping the forest. She treated us like a couple of red-headed stepchildren.

I wasn't that heartbroken when she died. Though there is no proof, I suspect Sean Palmer poisoned her for what she did to the two of you.

When she wiped Sean's memory, it was only of you. He was a good teacher; she wanted to keep him close and teach the followers and their children the coven's spells. If any of the children showed signs of having any magical ability, she would use them to her advantage to control the group even more.

I was outraged when I found out she had been having Sean teach Starleena from Death is the Beginning. *That book is dangerous, and I never wanted my daughter to work dark magic. I had little control but tried to protect my child, even if she was destined to be a guardian of the Shadow. After her death, Sean left the commune, and I suspect that is when he went to stay with Sun-Moon.*

Pittapat's spells had given the Shadow power. As she tried to gain its ability, it fed on her energy. She, Jaxson, and I were no longer strong enough to control it. We tried to identify another witch who would be able to join us. Starleena was not strong enough yet. It could reach its grasp outside the forest with less control over the Shadow.

We did not know the Shadow could reach anyone from its confinement until Starleena was taken. The Shadow called her to come to it, killing her once she was within its reach. Before the Shadow could trap her soul, her spirit came to me. Jaxson and I knew from the beginning that the Shadow had killed Starleena.

We tried to make it look as if she was missing. We were worried about the other members of the commune, especially the children. Jaxson came up with a plan to destroy the Shadow. A spell in Death is the Beginning *would send it back from where it came—essentially expelling it from our realm. Jaxson went alone to confront the Shadow. It was no match. The Shadow punished him severely for his betrayal before killing him.*

I found him and the book later that night. I hid the book in a tree trunk and took off. I was scared. The Shadow killed both my daughter and Jackson; it was only a matter of time before it came from. The Shadow will be freed from its jail if the power of the Circle is broken and all three guardian witches are dead.

I had to hide out until I could find two other witches with the power to see spirits who would be willing to join me to either dispel it from our realm or, at the very least, help me regain the power of the Circle of Eternal Shadow so we could confine it to the forest.

Armand is a member of the Circle; he is a low-level witch who wants to serve. Unfortunately, he does not have the power to see spirits and would not be able to ascend to be a part of the Witches Three. His power is to enhance other witches' powers. That is why your mother had him go to work for you. He was there to make sure her memory spell stayed intact.

When a witch dies, all their spells are broken. However, you are still under the memory spell. I am not sure why.

Armand is a powerful witch but not powerful enough to be one of the Shadow's guardians. He offered me sanctuary in his home and built a room in the basement to lock me in if the Shadow called for me. If I became under its power, I would be drawn to it and unable to stop myself. We tried to create a protection spell over the house so the Shadow could not find me, which is why the house looks like it does, with all the occult items everywhere.

Armand nor I have done anything illegal. You need to release me, or I am a dead woman. I can feel the pull of the shadow; it will find me, and even in jail, it will find a way to kill me."

Relda looked over at him and said, "You know, I am tired of all this hocus pocus bull shit; what the hell." Relda stormed out. This caused him to burst out laughing wildly.

His laughter filled the room, and Analee stared at him in bewilderment. After a moment, he managed to control his chuckles and wiped away a tear from the corner of his eye.

"Sorry about that," he said, still grinning. I'm just that this whole situation is so crazy. I don't know how to comprehend it completely; it's a bit bizarre." Analee raised an eyebrow, clearly not amused by his reaction. "Why are you acting like a fool? I know you know the truth. It's in your eyes. Who else have you spoken to?"

Crox Stiffened up, not sure how much to tell her.

"How do we stop it? Do you think it's even possible?" He said after he got himself under control.

Analee looked at him and said, "You have it in your blood. You can destroy this monster with my help, that is. We need to get out of here and meet up with Armand. She looked at him as if she were looking into his very soul. Her lips curled into an evil smile as she stated, "You are your mother's son."

Relda grabbed Crox by the arm and pulled him out of the interrogation room. She warned him that Armand had gotten a lawyer involved. "We cannot hold her unless we book her on something. I'm afraid there is nothing we can charge her with that will hold up in court."

"Can we put a tail on her?" Crox asked.

"Not unless we have probable cause she's going to commit a crime," Relda stated

With no other options, Relda had to release Analee from custody. Now that he knew where she lived, he decided to follow her. If what she said about the Shadow was true, she would not venture from Armand's house since they had created a protection barrier so the Shadow could not reach her.

Crox left the Sheriff's Office before Analee was discharged; he made the excuse to leave abruptly by telling Relda he had to meet a real estate client. He went out, got in his truck, and waited for Analee to leave. Not twenty minutes later, he saw Armand pull up in his white Mazda SUV and watched as Analee jumped in.

He followed them from a distance since Armand knew what his truck looked like. He couldn't believe this complex web of events that had unfolded before him, and he struggled to reconcile the logical and supernatural aspects of what was going on.

Crox kept his distance and observed as they pulled into Armand's seemingly ordinary house in a quiet suburban neighborhood. Even in the best neighborhoods, you never know what happens behind closed doors.

Once inside the house, Analee and Armand settled on the couch. Thankfully, they did not pull the front window curtains. He watched through binoculars as they discussed something fervently, their expressions serious with what looked like a touch of fear.

He wished he could hear their conversation but knew he had to tread carefully. If he was going to take any action, he needed to be sure of his next steps.

As night settled, Crox saw Armand get up and close the curtains. He knew he could not risk getting any closer, so he decided to leave and make another stop before going home. Crox parked in front of Galinda the Good Witch: Books, Curiosities, and Notions. He wondered if Sun-Moon would talk with him again after he helped her get arrested.

His heart raced as he entered the occult shop. The tinkling of a bell announced his arrival, and he spotted Sun—Moon behind the counter, sorting through a stack of old, weathered books.

"Hello again," he said, attempting a friendly smile. "How's it shaking?"

Sun-Moon slammed the book she was looking at on the counter and glared at him. "What the hell do you want now? Come for more answers, have you? The local library is down the street."

Crox steadied himself; he knew Sun-Moon had a reason to be upset with him. However, he did need more answers. He had heard twice now that he had been in a relationship with Sean Palmer.

As far as Crox could remember, he hadn't even dated in years, so what was it with the man who broke into his house and shot Jax?

"Yes, I do have questions, and I expect answers. I will not leave here until you tell me what you know about me and Sean Palmer."

An oddly bright smile crossed Sun-Moon's lips as she said, "You are ready to regain your memory. I can tell you all about your love affair with my brother Sean. You see, I have known you for years. But had to carry on the charade, lest your mother feed me to the Shadow."

Chapter 16

SEARCH FOR MEMORY

Our memories and past experiences shape us into the individuals we are. But what happens if some of those memories are lost? Would our predetermined fate also be altered?

"Do you remember me before you entered this store two weeks ago? I have plenty of memories of you." Sun-Moon said to Crox teasingly.

Crox's eyes narrowed, his gaze sweeping over the strange-looking woman. He couldn't recall ever seeing her before, and her unique sense of style and appearance would have stood out in his memory if they had crossed paths. His voice was flat and unimpressed as he spoke, conveying his skepticism. "No, I don't remember you."

Sun-Moon laughed hard. "Yes, I have a unique style. But we are not here to talk about fashion now, are we?"

Sun-Moon stood up and approached a huge multi-colored cabinet behind her sales counter. She reached into her bra and brought out an old antique brass key. As she turned the key, Crox could hear the lock click as if it did not want to open its door and show the secrets it kept hidden inside.

She reached into the cabinet and retrieved a vanilla folder and a blue crystal decanter. Her expression turned serious as she handed the folder to him and said. "These are some of the memories missing from your mind. I am giving them to you because I believe you should know the truth, especially since a difficult task is ahead of you. Perhaps it will help you fulfill your destiny."

Crox took the folder hesitantly, his fingers brushing over the aged paper, and asked, "What's in here?"

"Your past," Sun-Moon replied. "It Contains photos of events, relationships, and encounters removed from your memory. They might help bring back what your mother took away from you."

Crox opened the folder and began to skim through its contents. There were photographs, handwritten notes, and even old newspaper clippings. One photo caught Crox's attention immediately: a picture of him with Sean Palmer. They looked like friends, even close friends, standing side by side with enormous smiles on their faces, suggesting genuine intimacy between them.

"Sean Palmer," Crox muttered, his brow furrowing as he stared at the picture. Why can't I remember him?" He tried hard to reach into his mind for any memory of knowing this man in the photo. As hard as he tried, nothing came to him.

Crox saw himself almost hugging the man in the picture, which he had no memory of; this man was a stranger. Except for seeing him shoot Jax and then seeing him at the police station, he had no other recollection of ever seeing Sean Palmer.

Sun-Moon watched with patience as Crox struggled mentally with what he was seeing. She poured some of the blue liquid from the crystal decanter into a small shot glass and handed it to him. "Drink this. It's a potion that will help jog your memory. It won't restore everything instantly, but it might help you reconnect with some of your lost moments." She stated.

Crox took the glass and looked at the blue liquid, swirling it around like an expensive wine. He hesitated for a moment and smelled the concoction, but it had no smell at all. He then downed the potion in one gulp. It had a bitter and sweet taste, leaving a tingling sensation in his mouth and burning as it went down his throat. For a quick moment, he thought he was being poisoned.

Crox placed the glass back on the counter, feeling a strange sensation in his mind like a fog lifting away. Fragments of memories started to surface—conversations, laughter, moments spent with Sean. Crox began to recall a small apartment, the two embracing romantically. A rush of sadness took hold of him as if he were seeing the ghost of a deceased loved one. As quickly as the sensations and memories came, they vanished from his mind just as fast. He left only the feelings; the memories were all gone.

"You and Sean were more than just friends," Sun-Moon said softly, her eyes fixed on his face as if she could read his thoughts. You two were lovers."

"I think I had a flash of a memory, but it's gone now. What happened?" Crox stated, a bit confused.

Sun-Moon looked down at her feet and sighed, "I am sorry; I can only bring back memories in flashes with motion. I do not have the power to make them stay. The power of memory manipulation is a complex spell, and the one your mother used on you was stronger than the one she used on Sean."

"How can we break this spell?" Crox asked.

"With the help of Analee and Armand, the last two remaining witches of the Circle of the Eternal Shadow, along with a spell from your mother's grimoire, it can be done." Sun-Moon continued, "I will try to plan a meeting at Armand's place. Analee won't leave the house unless necessary. I know Armand is still pissed at you for firing him, but deep down, he has to understand why you did it. I'll make the arrangements and call you when they are ready to talk to you."

Crox left the shop and headed home with nothing else to do. He would have to bring Jax up to date since Analee's story matched his. He felt he could now trust the feline again.

Arriving at his house, Crox was greeted by Jax, who meowed and rubbed against his legs. He crouched down to pet the cat, his mind still racing."Jax, I think I need to have a serious talk with you," he said, looking into the feline's eyes as if searching for answers. He proceeded to recount his meeting with Sun-Moon and Analee.

"Have you found my Analee?" Crox heard in his mind. He answered, "Yes, she is staying with Armand, my office manager."

Jax turned around in multiple circles as if chasing his tail. He was excited. Crox had spilled everything he knew over the last few days to Jax. In his heart, he knew that all that Jax and Analee had told him was true.

His mother had once tried to save him from the Shadow's grasp, but then he teamed up with the creature to turn him over to it and let his soul be trapped by the thing for eternity.

A hatred he had never felt suddenly took over him. His mother, the one who gave him life, wanted to take it for her power gain. Crox realized even his family and close friends could never be fully trusted. He had been lied to for years by both.

Later in the evening, back at home, as Crox was preparing dinner for himself and Jax, the phone rang; it was Relda. She called to let him know he was seen sitting in front of Armand's house. It seemed a patrol car had been patrolling the neighborhood, watching the house, and saw him. Relda strongly urged him not to stalk Analee or Armand. He agreed and advised Relda of his meeting with Sun-Moon and how she is attempting to set up a get-together with them. Relda suggested not meeting with them alone and calling her once he heard if they agreed to meet with him.

Sun-Moon contacted him a few hours later, as promised, and informed him that Analee and Armand were willing to talk. The meeting would take place in a few days at Armand's house, where they had a protection spell placed from the Shadow's reach. It was clear that Shadow's power was getting more robust, and Armand wanted to ensure they would be safe. They also wanted a couple of days to prepare. He asked if Relda could join in. There was no objection as long she was coming as a friend and not in the capacity of Sheriff.

After speaking with Sun-Moon, Crox drove to his office and grabbed his mother's book from his safe. Holding *Death is the Beginning, and h*e felt a strange sensation wash over him. It was almost like a suspicion that he was in danger and might very well die soon.

Crox took the spell book home and put it under his pillow when he went to bed. That night, he slept like a rock with no dreams. His sleep was that of a dead man, his mind entirely still for the first time in months.

The next afternoon, Crox found himself with Jax standing outside Armand's house with Jax at his side, his heart pounding with a mixture of anticipation and anxiety. He did not know what to expect from this gathering, but he knew it was a pivotal moment that could shape the direction of his life, even the possibility of his death.

Relda arrived shortly after, dressed casually. As she approached the porch, she smiled reassuringly at him."Ready for this?" she asked, her eyes showing excitement and concern.

Crox nodded, his gaze fixed on the door before him. "As ready as I'll ever be."

Crox knocked on the door and was surprised that Sun-Moon answered. "Hello, you two, or should I say three? Hello, Jaxson," she said as she looked down at the cat.

Sun-Moon, who had brought them here, stood near the entrance with a knowing smile. "They are preparing a space of protection and will be with us soon," she whispered to him and Relda.

Crox looked at Relda, who gave him an encouraging nod. The tension in the air was thick as they waited for Analee and Armand to join them. After what felt like an eternity, the basement door swung open, revealing Analee, her eyes weak with weariness. Armand followed close behind her, his expression filled with frustration. Jax ran up to Analee, rubbing her around her legs and purring loudly. She looked down at the cat with recognition, picking him up and kissing him on the head, a lonely tear rolling down her left cheek.

Crox heard Jax telepathically. *"She can't hear me; only you can. I love and miss her and am sorry for going after the Shadow alone, which got me killed."*

"Hello, Analee, Armand," Crox greeted them, his voice steady but tinged with uncertainty. He ignored Jax's request. "Thank you for agreeing to meet us. I'm hoping we can come up with a plan that can be beneficial to us all."

"I see you brought the book. That is going to be a big help." Analee stated.

Armand asked them all to join him in the basement. He advised that this is where his protection spell is the most powerful. There, they would be able to examine the book's spells safely.

"The first thing I want to do is get my memory back. Do you think you two can do that?" Crox asked through pursed lips.

Armand's gaze remained fixed on him, his eyes hard. "You fired me; now you want my help."

"You have lied to me since you came to work for me. You deserved to be fired. You are lucky I did not shoot you." Crox said in a rush.

"Touché," was Armand's only response as they walked down the steps to the basement to the secret room Analee was staying in.

Inside the basement's secret room, the atmosphere seemed to change. The air felt thicker, almost charged with electric energy. The room was dimly lit, with shelves filled with crystals, animal bones, and old books lining the walls. In the center of the room was a large, round table covered with a deep crimson red cloth. Analee motioned for everyone to take a seat.

Crox, Relda, and Sun-Moon settled around the table while Armand took his place standing next to Analee. Jax sat at Crox's feet. Analee stood at the head of the table. Her eyes focused on the old spell book Crox had brought with him.

"We need to be cautious," Analee began, her voice soft but determined. The spells within that book are powerful but can also be very dangerous. We don't know the full extent of what your mother did to you or if undoing her actions will have any repercussions."

Crox nodded silently, absorbing her words. He was eager to reclaim his memories but fully understood the risks involved. Armand spoke up, breaking the silence. "Before we attempt anything, we should strengthen the protection spell around this space. The Shadow's influence is growing, and we don't want it eavesdropping on our actions."

Analee agreed, and together, they chanted a spell in a language Crox didn't understand. The room seemed to shimmer as Armand and Analee chanted. When they were through, Analee stated they were safe to proceed.

Crox inhaled deeply and gazed at the grimoire of spells before him. "Let's begin with my memories. Can you utilize the incantations in this book to assist me in recalling what my mother stole from me?"

Analee and Armand exchanged a glance before nodding. She gestured for the book, which he reluctantly handed over to her. She turned to a page, and a small smile graced her lips. She took hold of Armand's hand, and they began to chant.

Crox closed his eyes, his mind reaching out, willing the spell to work. He felt a gentle tugging sensation, like a thread being pulled, and then suddenly, his mind was flooded with images. Memories rushed back to him. Armand and Annalee's voices began harmonizing a strange, song-like melody.

He began seeing snippets of his childhood, then his teenage years, followed by his life with Sean Palmer, Jaxson, and Analee. Then, the realization that he, too, was a member of the Circle of the Eternal Shadow. But as suddenly as they came, the memories faded, slipping through his grasp like water.

His eyes shot open. Crox clutched his head in frustration. "No, wait! They're slipping away!" Analee and Armand ceased their chanting. "I'm sorry," Analee said softly. The memories are trying to reestablish themselves, but the spell's grip on them is strong. We need to find a way to weaken the hold of your mother's magick."

Crox took a few deep breaths, struggling to compose himself. He glanced over at Relda, who was watching him with concern. "We can't give up now, guys," he said. We must find a way to break this spell once and for all."

Armand interjected, "There might be a way, but it's risky. We could attempt to confront your mother's spirit directly in the realm between and death to seek help in removing the spell."

"But what if the Shadow has her soul? Then her spirit cannot come forth." Sun-Moon chimed in.

Relda's eyes widened, and she exchanged a worried glance with him. "Is that safe? Didn't your mother want to give you to the Shadow?"

Analee replied," She is now dead and can no longer harm anyone. In death, she may want to correct what she did in life.

The spell will not be easy, and it carries its own set of dangers. But if we want to sever the connection between his mother's magic and his memories, it might be our best option.

"Let's get-ter done; I'm ready," Crox replied.

Chapter 17

Call the Spirit

Analee and Armand excused themselves to retrieve the items needed to evoke a spirit of the dead. Upon returning to the table, Armand had a live chicken he had retrieved from the backyard with him, and he placed the animal before them.

With a swift, practiced hand, Annalee carefully poured the contents of a jar onto the wooden table, creating a circle with the white grains of salt. In the center of this circle sat the plump chicken, its feathers ruffled and eyes wide with fear. Armand approached the creature with a silver knife, similar to the one Crox had uncovered at the commune.

Without hesitation, Aemand raised the blade and swiftly cut the chicken's throat, causing it to squawk and flail in its final moments. The metallic scent of blood filled the air as the life drained from the animal into the circle of salt, turning the white salt red.

The deep, crimson lifeblood gushed from the chicken on the table before them, cascading over the edges and staining the white carpet. Relda's scream pierced through the air like a banshee wail, her eyes wide with horror and disgust as she looked upon the gruesome scene before her. Her mind raced, trying to comprehend why anyone would do such a thing. The metallic scent of blood filled her nostrils, making her stomach churn in disgust. She could hardly believe that this was happening right in front of her.

They paid no attention to her outburst as they began to chant in low, rhythmic tones, their voices becoming one strange but mesmerizing melody. The room seemed to vibrate. Crox felt a tingling sensation on his forearms. He clenched his fists, fear surging within him. He suddenly felt the fullness of his bladder.

As the chanting reached a fevered pitch, the room seemed to flicker with a strange white light. The air crackled with electric energy, and a gust of wind swept through the room, extinguishing the candles lit on the sideboard. The table started to shake as the hairs on Crox's neck rose, and then he felt an invisible hand on his shoulder. That is when Crox's bladder released itself, covering him in his own waste.

A form began to take shape and rise from within the center of the circle of salt and blood on the table. It was a translucent figure, shimmering in the room's dim light. Crox recognized the figure before him—his mother, Pittapat.

Analee spoke to the ghostly shape of his mother, "How do we break the memory spell you placed on your son."

The ghostly shape ignored the question and locked eyes with Crox. "My dear boy. I need your help. The powerful darkness of the Shadow's grip has me trapped. I cannot pass on to the other side."

"How can I help you if I can't fully remember who I am? You took a part of my life away and then wanted to give me to the Shadow. It seems you got what you deserve." Crox stated

Pittapat spoke again; Crox heard the regret in her voice. "I was desperate. I thought I was protecting you from the Shadow's wrath. But I was wrong. It consumed me, twisted my intentions."

Crox clenched his fists, his emotions roiling within him. "You were my mother. How could you betray me like this?"

The spirit's form wavered as if struggling to maintain its presence. "I am trapped. The Shadow's hold is strong. But I still may be able to help and guide you in destroying it. All you need is in my spell book. There is a reason I named *Death is the Beginning*; it is because once we die, our souls are transferred to another realm I call the home base, and there, you can choose to come back to this realm and correct your past mistakes and become a better being, or you can pass on to your final salvation once you are finally ready and truly the best you can be. This can take hundreds of years of being reincarnated."

Pittapat continued, "The Shadow has trapped mine and other souls; it feeds off our pain and sorrow of being unable to cross over. We are earthbound spirits. When the Shadow is busy attempting to bring other souls to the forest, the trapped ones who are strong enough to reach out to the living who can see spirits do so, seeking help. However, if it finds we are doing this, we suffer even more. Starleena suffers now. The Shadow realized she was speaking to Jax."

Crox leaned forward, his voice filled with desperation. "Tell me, Mother, how can I break the spell? How can I regain my memories?"

The spirit's gaze held as she spoke, her words fading in and out like a distant echo. "The book—it holds the key. Find the passage that speaks of the Shadow's pact. Find the amulet of lost souls. It has a part of my spirit attached to it. Long ago, I found a spell to split my soul to keep a part of me earthbound when I died."

Crox's mind raced, processing the information. "But how do I destroy the Shadow?"

Pittapat's voice grew fainter, her form beginning to fade. "Use the spell in the book, go to the forest, complete the circle, and bring back what escaped the Shadow clutches. My son, remember I loved you, even in my darkest moments."

Pittapat seemed to materialize out of thin air, but just as quickly, she vanished, and her presence dissipated into the atmosphere. The room was left in an unsettling stillness, only interrupted by Crox's heavy breathing. The scent of urine permeated the air.

Relda's hand gently covered Crox's, her fingers intertwining with his. Concern filled her features as she asked, "Are you alright?" He turned to her, tears shimmering in his eyes. They were a reflection of the pain and turmoil he had been through. "I know what I must do now," he said quietly, his voice heavy with emotion. "But first, I need a hot shower to wash away the dirt and grime, a change of clothes to feel human again, and a stiff drink to numb my mind." Relda nodded understandingly.

Crox asked Armand to use his shower to clean up while Relda returned to his house to retrieve a pair of clean pants. He also asked her to bring him a necklace from his bedroom side table. The one Sun-Moon had given him, shaped like a cat with horns. He was positive this must be the amulet his mother had stated had a part of her soul attached to it and would be needed to stop the Shadow.

Twenty minutes later, Relda returned just as he got out of the shower and toweled off. She brought with her both items he had asked for. Once in fresh, clean clothes, Crox went downstairs to the basement, where everyone was still assembled and waiting for him.

"Alright, then, folks, we have the book as well as the amulet. Let's see if we can regain my memory," Crox burst out.

"How? Pittapat never told us. We are still at a loss on how to break her spell." declared Armand.

Analee jumped from her chair, snatching the necklace from his hands, and said, through manic laughs, "I know what we need to do! We need to separate her soul from the necklace. And I know just how to do it."

Analee's sudden enthusiasm caught everyone off guard. She seemed like a woman possessed. "Separating a soul from an object is complex, but I can do it with a spell from *Death is the Beginning*."

Relda asked Analee, "Are you sure you know what you're doing?"

Analee looked at Relda as a parent does to a small child who just asked a stupid question. Without even acknowledging her question, Analee went to work on the spell. First, they had to clean up the dead chicken's blood.

Analee instructed everyone to gather around the table where she had the book open. She turned to a page from the middle of the book and laid the necklace on it. She then started reciting a spell from the grimoire in a strange language. As she chanted, her hands moved gracefully over the book's page, her fingers tracing symbols and patterns that began glowing with a purple light rising from the necklace.

The atmosphere in the room grew tense as her chanting continued. The air seemed to thicken, much like when Pittapat's spirit had appeared. Crox felt another rush of electric energy coursing through him, and he hoped his bladder would hold this time. He also saw the others seemingly bracing themselves for whatever was about to happen. Analee's voice reached a fevered pitch as a blinding light erupted from the book's pages. The light enveloped the necklace on the book, and for a moment, Crox felt a sharp jolt of pain in his head just behind his left temple.

As the light subsided, Crox felt the pain go away. A strange vibration started emanating from the necklace as if something was attempting to break away from it. They all watched in awe as a smokey figure emerged from the necklace, hovering in the air before them. It was his mother's soul, as it separated from the cat amulet.

The smoky figure looked around, its features shifting and swirling as if trying to regain its form. He stared at his mother's misty outline, still struggling to comprehend what was happening.

Analee's voice filled the room again, softer and more soothing. She began to chant a different incantation that seemed to guide his mother's soul. The figure started to take on a more solid form, and as it did, Analee grabbed the silver knife and plugged it into Pittapat's semi-solid form. A howl of pain filled the room as the form vanished.

The cries of pain from his mother's spirit still rang in Crox's ears as the room's light grew brighter. The heaviness in the air lifted away in the aftermath of the intense magic that had been unleashed.

Analee stood there, panting slightly, the silver knife still in her hand. She looked drained. "I did it. I separated her soul from the amulet.

Relda and Armand just sat there with bewildered expressions. *Jax jumped onto his lap and telepathically said, "We are one step closer." They can now redo the memory spell for you, and this time, it will work.*

Crox's mind was a whirlwind of sadness and joy, knowing his mother was now truly gone. Her soul entirely belonged to the Shadow. He looked down at the cat with horns amulet on the table. It was free of the small piece of his mother's soul that had once inhabited it.

"Analee," he managed to say, his voice shaky. Now that the connection is broken, can you do the spell again to regain my memories?"

Analee looked at him with a smile and nodded slowly, taking a deep breath to steady herself. "Yes, now that her soul is completely severed from this realm, we can attempt the memory spell again. But this time, I believe it will work, but we need to take a break; I need to recharge."

"Can we try again tomorrow?" asked Armand.

This spell seemed to have taken a toll on everyone, and the idea of postponing his attempt to regain his memories was met with a sigh of relief for everyone except Crox.

Crox still wanted to move forward. Unfortunately, the rest of the group requested to gather again the next day to proceed with the memory spell, so he had no choice but to wait.

The basement room slowly emptied as Sun-Moon, Armand, and Analee went upstairs. Relda sat silently, watching him as he stared down at the table where the amulet lay. Its glow had diminished, and it looked like any other piece of jewelry.

Still on his lap, Jax said, "It still holds immense power; put it around your neck, and don't take it off." Crox smiled faintly as he looked down at his feline brother."Alright, I'll wear it," he said, wrapping the necklace around his neck.

"Should you be wearing that thing? Is it safe?" Relda asked

Crox just shrugged as he got up and headed upstairs to leave. He was starting to feel exhaustion take over him and just wanted to go home and get into bed. He didn't want to talk anymore.

Relda drove him and Jax home, and they sat in silence. Relda was not sure what to think of all she had just witnessed. She felt she had seen a murder in some sense, both the chicken and the partial spirit of Pittapat Diamond. If she was to tell what had happened to the district attorney, not only would she lose her job, she would find herself in a mental institution locked up with the key thrown away.

Relda dropped him and Jax at their front door and proceeded to her home. She told them she would be back tomorrow to pick them up and return to Armand's.

Crox opened two cans of tuna fish. He put one on the floor for Jax, then sat on the couch and ate the other out of the can with a spoon.

After the hearty dinner, Crox grabbed a cigar and bottle of Jack Daniels for dessert and headed out to his back deck, enjoying the Cuban while getting plastered. Later, he staggered to the couch and passed out. Jax jumped beside him, settling down on his chest, purring softly. Sleep would come peacefully to Jax, but he would not be so lucky. This dream would either prepare him for what would come or be a premonition of his death if he failed to defeat the Shadow.

Chapter 18

Memory Restored

Darkness was all around him. Crox turned and turned but saw nothing. He put his hand before his face but couldn't see it. He had no idea where he was. Crox let out a scream, but it fell flat in the void of the darkness. Something was here with him; he could feel its presence even if he could not see it. The air was cool, and he started to shiver involuntarily. Any happiness he had within him drained away as if an unseen vampire was sucking it out of him.

A deep, hoarse voice echoed from the shadows, declaring, "You belong to me now. You won't escape me a second time. I will thrive on your suffering for eternity." It was the Shadow speaking.

Crox felt like he was falling to the ground, so he shut his eyes tight. The sensation soon passed, and when he opened his eyes, he found himself in the meadow under the large oak tree, in the grassy meadow. His cousin Danny stood there watching him with large, sad eyes, a single tear rolling down his left cheek.

This dream was like none he had ever experienced. He had felt the coldness of the darkness but now felt the sun's warmth on his face beaming down from the bright blue sky. Even the tree he stood under looked more real than it ever had in his past dreams. The bark from the trunk was rough and brittle under his fingers. Had he ever touched the tree before in his prior dreams? He wasn't sure.

Crox embraced his cousin, feeling the strength of his hug; this was more than a dream. Danny was truly here with him. Where were they? He became scared and started trembling.

Danny broke the silence, Sensing his fear, "Don't worry, cuz you're safe now. I have you. It started as a dream but is more than a dream. You have been brought to a holding realm between earthbound and crossing over to the other side. This place is also where the Shadow lives. When I was crossed over from the dream state, the Shadow got to you first. However, I was able to grab you before it had a chance to trap you."

Crox stumbled over his words, his breath catching in his throat. "H-How...h-how is this...possible?" he stuttered, his eyes wide with disbelief.

Danny's expression remained stoic as he delivered the unsettling truth. "When you die, you ascend to another realm where earthly restrictions no longer bind you. I have the ability to move between these realms with the aid of seers and witches."

Crox felt a cold chill run down his spine at Danny's words. He couldn't believe what he was hearing. "S-so, what does this mean for me? Am I stuck here in this in-between place?" His voice trembled with fear and confusion.

Danny smiled warmly, his eyes filled with sadness and love. "No, Cuz. You're not stuck here. This is a transitional space. I brought you here with the help of a seer to help guide you in the fight you will soon face."

"What seer? Is it Analee, Armand, or Sun-Moon?" Crox asked.

"In time, you will find out. You will soon have your memories back now that Pittapat's spirit is no longer earthbound. Your memories will start to flood back to you, and you will regain your power."

"Wait a minute, What Power?" Crox said, confused.

"My dear cousin, you are a witch and seer of spirits. You can see spirits in your dreams like you do with me. Pittapat tried to take that power away from you when she used the memory spell. I, however, was also a witch in life, and since we are blood, I found a way past her spell to come to you.

All these years of dreaming of me was not a dream. I had to come to you while you were in a dream state to talk with you. I have been able to watch over you from the spirit realm. When your memories come back, you will understand. You have a special power that your mother was jealous of and wanted for herself. Please don't be mad at me or the other Circle of the Eternal Shadow members. We were all looking to protect you against your mother's plans."

Crox's voice was laced with uncertainty as he asked, "What about Vonda? Did I know her before my memory was taken from me? Can I trust her?"

"Vonda knew of you but did not meet you until after your memory was taken. She loves you and only wants to protect you. Vonda was a coven member but wasn't in the inner circle of the Witches Three. After I died, I called out to her and asked her to watch over you; she is a seer of spirits. With her help, you will be able to defeat the Shadow and save the souls of many."

"I don't know how to defeat this thing. I don't even know where to begin."Crox pleaded

Danny grabbed his hand, placed it on his chest, and said, "All you need is here, in your heart. You will have help. Go to the commune; it has been blessed and has the most protection from the Shadow. Bring all those you need to the property to help you. As your memories return, you will know what to do. Trust in yourself, Cuz. One final thing: never take off that necklace you are wearing, and always keep the knife you found at the commune on you."

Crox found himself all of a sudden back in the darkness. He heard laughter all around him. Then he felt pain in his chest, a sharp sticking pain as if he were having a heart attack. He awoke with Jax sitting on his chest, kneading him with his sharp claws digging into his chest.

In his mind, Crox heard the cat say, "Welcome back, my brother. I hope your trip to the other side was beneficial. Now feed me." He then jumped down and ran into the kitchen.

Crox sat at the edge of the couch, his head throbbing with pain. It was far worse than any hangover he had experienced before. The dream he had just woken up from lingered in his mind, but he couldn't be sure if it was indeed a dream.

What did Jax say? Welcome back. Crox tried to make sense of what Danny had told him, but his thoughts were still foggy.

Crox could still feel the chill of the dark place from his dream and shuddered at the memory. That was one place he never wanted to return to.

Croc glanced at his phone. 11:00 a.m. He hadn't slept that late in years. Slowly dragging himself to the kitchen, he found Jax waiting patiently by the fridge for his breakfast. Crox grabbed an old iron skillet that had been passed down in his family for over three decades and began cooking up some well-seasoned scrambled eggs and turkey sausage for himself and Jax.

As Crox placed the skillet on the stove and turned on the heat, a memory flashed in his mind; it was of him and Sean Plamermaking dinner together using this very skillet. They had danced together in this very kitchen while they prepared their meal, listening to Elton John's "The Bitch is Back."He staggered back at the forcefulness of the memory overtook him. Jax stared at him with a knowing look on his little feline face.

His heart raced as the memory flooded his mind. Croc could see Sean's face and hear his laughter. He remembered the way Sean used to playfully splash water on him as they cooked together. The image was so vivid and real that he could almost reach out and touch it. He felt the warmth of their connection, the love they shared.

Tears welled up in his eyes as he tried to process the overwhelming emotions that this memory brought back to him. He realized his memories were returning, just as Danny had said they would. It was like a dam had burst, and a torrent of forgotten moments rushed back to him in a flood. The pain of losing his memories and the people he had forgotten crushed him.

Jax rubbed against his legs, offering a comforting presence. He bent down and scooped the cat into his arms, holding him tightly and kissing his head.

"Thank you, Danny," Crox whispered to himself. He knew that with his cousin's guidance had opened the floodgates of his memories, allowing him to reconnect with the past and prepare him for what was to come.

Crox found himself lost in happy and sad memories as the day wore on. He remembered moments with his family and even the times he had spent at the Commune with Jaxson and his mother. He realized that each memory was a piece of the puzzle, a part of his identity that he had lost. With each memory that returned, he felt a sense of inner power brewing within him.

Relda arrived later that afternoon, finding Crox lost in thought on his couch. She looked concerned as she approached him. "Are you okay?" she asked gently.

He looked up at her, his eyes filled with excitement. "Relda, my memories are coming back and so much more," Crox said with conviction.

Relda's eyes widened in surprise. "Really? That's incredible!"

Crox nodded, a bittersweet smile forming on his lips. "Yeah, it's like I'm Reliving moments from my past. It's a little overwhelming. I realize I have an inner power, the strength that was taken from me."

She smiled warmly. "I always have known you were strong. We're in this together; whatever you need, I'm here for you."

"Thank you. Your friendship means the world to me." Crox realized he no longer mistrusted Relda. If she turned out to be a cult member of the Circle of the Eternal Shadow, he knew she had not been working with his mother to give him over to the Shadow.

Relda sat down next to him on the couch. "So, what's the plan now? With your memories returning, how can we confront and defeat this Shadow thing?"

Crox smiled wide and looked at her, laughing, "Not a damn clue, Boo." He leaned back, deep in thought. "In my dream state, I'm not even sure it was that, but anyway, my cousin Danny mentioned the Commune as a place of protection from the Shadow. He also told me to gather allies and trust in myself.

"This necklace that mother had cursed with a portion of her soul I'm wearing, Crox said that I should never take off, and the knife I found near Jacob's trailer that I need to keep on me."

Relda's brow furrowed. "That's a lot to take in, but I'm progressing as best I can. We should go to the Commune. It can be our new base of operations. Maybe Analee and the others can help us understand more, plus your mother's spell book should help."

Crox contacted Analee and invited her to join them at the Commune, where they would use Jaxson's trailer as their base. Analee was unsure about leaving the safety of Armand's house, but Crox reminded her that the Shadow was becoming more powerful and she couldn't hide forever. As Crox recovered his memories, he also discovered his ability to sense the Shadow and track its movements. The energy emanating from it was faint but steadily growing stronger.

Crox then called Sun-Moon at her shop and got her voicemail, so he left a detailed account of his plans and asked her to come to the Commune the following evening. He wasn't sure if Armand and Analee would come, but he was sure Sun-Moon would.

After Relda left, he packed a duffle bag of clothes and gathered up Jax's food and litter box. Crox knew he would be at the Commune for some time. He was starting to trust the inner feelings he was having. Crox also knew the ghost of Starleena was nearby; even though he could not see or hear her, he knew she was talking to Jax.

Starleena was there; she and Jax were in an intense conversation. She was agitated. "Don't bring my mom back to the forest. The Shadow hasn't stopped calling for her. It is waiting now. The thing knows Crox has gotten his power back; the two are connected, and it knows he will come to it. If you take Mom, she may die at the Shadow's hand and be stuck here like me."

Jax was fully aware of the danger his child's mother would face. He had loved Analee, but they were not in love. When they met, they had a job to do: to have Starleena so she would have his blood for his mother's evil plans. He did want to protect Analee and Crox, but his desire to release his daughter from the grip of the Shadow was much stronger. He would sacrifice both of them if it meant saving his child.

Later that morning, Crox loaded Jax and the overnight bag to head to the commune, the 20-acre property he now owned. As he locked his front door, Crox felt he would never return to his house in Fredericksburg. Once at the old house once owned by his familiar and half-brother Jaxson, now known as Jax, he felt at home. Jax jumped onto a recliner to let Crox know this was his seat.

The memories that continued to flood back were both a gift and a challenge. Each recollection brought with it strong emotions. Crox was Jaxson's older brother, but Jaxson was the one gifted, both with seeing spirits and the power to control the Shadow.

Jaxson was destined to be part of the Witches Three. Crox did not have his abilities. As the memories flooded him, Crox understood he was the weakest in supernatural ability in his family. Perhaps this is why his mother eventually offered him up to the Shadow.

On his way to his new home, Crox had stopped at Popeye's to get a box of spicy chicken. He tore into it as if he hadn't eaten in days. Jax enjoyed a can of tuna. After dinner, Crox browsed *Death is the Beginning*. He was starting to understand some of the writings and spells. Now, with most of his memory back, he knew he was a witch, even if just a minor one.

His goal for the evening was to find the spell needed to destroy the Shadow or send it away so he would be free of it. The book was thick, and seeing what he needed would take time and concentration. Jax sat and watched from his recliner. The cat remained silent while they ate, and Crox went through the spell book.

Crox busied himself cleaning up the old house the next day and getting ready for Armand and Analee. Sun-Moon and Relda would also be there. Though Crox needed his friend Relda, he could have done without Sun-Moo. Crox stood outside the trailer smoking a cigar as the sun descended behind the trees, looking out at the forest beyond the property, deep in thought.

Analee and Armand had arrived earlier in the day, and now Sun-Moon was coming up the drive. It looked like she had a passenger with her. As the white Honda Civic approached the trailer, he saw the passenger: the Vonderful Vonda.

Chapter 19

THE CIRCLE

Vonda? What was she doing here? Why in the hell did Sun-Moon bring her to the commune? What good would she be? Crox said to himself angrily.

Crox's frustration simmered just below the surface as he watched Vonda gracefully step out of the car. Sensing his unease, Jax hopped down from his throne – the recliner – and followed Crox outside to observe the approaching women. The sun beat down mercilessly on the gravel rock driveway, casting harsh shadows that stretched across their path like claws. Crox clenched his fists, trying to contain his growing annoyance. Vonda's flowing dress fluttered in the breeze, giving her an almost virginal appearance. Jax let out a low growl, mirroring Crox's tension. As they drew closer, Crox could see Vonda's determination and knew she would not back down easily.

Sun-Moon walked up, leaving Vonda by the car, and said, with a reassuring smile, "I know you might be a bit surprised to see Vonda with me but hear me out. She will be able to help us. You will need other Circle of the Eternal Shadow members to have a chance against the Shadow. Vonda can get them back here. She is, after all, very persuasive."

Crox walked over to Vonda and said, "You better be here to help defeat this thing; if I start to think otherwise, I'll shoot you dead myself."

Vonda appeared unfazed by his statement. She said, "I love you and will die to protect you. Trust me, everything I have done was for you; even if you don't see it now, you will." Crox gave her a scornful look, turned, and headed back inside. Jax followed close behind him.

Inside, Analee and Armand studied the spell book, arguing who they should call to help from the now-disbanded coven. Sun-Moon sat in the corner, drinking beer, with a bored look on her face, watching them argue as if it were a tennis match.

After a lull in the heated conversation, Sun-Moon spoke up, "You are going to need five people to complete the sacred circle and will need as many members of the Circle to be here at the property chanting a protection spell to provide some protection from the Shadow, social everyone."

Crox sighed and ran his fingers through his hair, clearly frustrated with the situation. "Fine, we'll call in the members. But I want to clarify that I don't want anyone risking their life. This is my fight." Cox's gaze shifted from Analee to Armand, then finally to Vonda and Sun-Moon. He could feel the weight of this nightmare resting heavily on his shoulders. "Let's get going,"

Vonda and Armand got on their cell phones and called the Circle of the Eternal Shadow members, asking them to come to the Commune as soon as possible.

While they made the calls, Analee and Sun-Moon reviewed the spell needed to call forth the Shadow. They sat in the kitchen, not sure what to do. Jax, on the other hand, knew what he needed to do. The cat ran out the door and headed out to the forest. Jax was going to throw the first stone in this fight. He would draw the Shadow away from the souls it held as prisoners. They could join the battle with the Shadow distracted, even if they had little power as spirits. They would need all the help possible.

As Jax raced off to the forest, Relda received a call from the police station. There had been a break-in at Armand's house. The Sheriff's department had a couple of deputies at the home now. Since Relda still had an open investigation on Armand, they wanted her to know and see if she wanted to check out the scene. Relda told Armand, and the two jumped up to go. She told him not to do anything until they returned. Crox promised to sit tight.

Analee looked at Crox after Relda and Armand had left, saying, "We don't need her here. What will she do, arrest an entity from another realm?"

"She has been helping me from the beginning; she is also my friend. I trust her and need her by my side," Crox said flatly.

Relda and Armand reached Crox's house, finding it overturned and ransacked. If Relda didn't know better, she would have assumed Vonda had done it. The place was a wreck, but nothing seemed to be missing.

After the deputies left, Armand told Relda that an antique silver knife had been taken. It was the one used to kill the chicken when they cast the spell to bring forth Pittapat. The knife would be needed to do the spell he planned to use to destroy the Shadow. Without it, the spell wouldn't work.

Back in the forest, Jax reached the edge of where the Shadow dwelled, his heart pounding in his feline chest. He could sense the darkness lurking within the trees, the same evil force that had once held him captive. The cat knew he had to confront it, to lure it away from its captives without getting himself killed again.

Jax stepped deeper into the woods, remembering his fear of when the Shadow had trapped him, feeding off his pain. He put the fear aside as it would do him no good; he needed to be strong. The sky seemed to grow darker and cloudy and had no stars shining down to provide him light. However, with his feline eyes, he could see in the darkness. Jax moved forward through the trees; he could feel the presence of the Shadow. Jax would have to get its attention.

Taking a deep breath, Jax let out a loud, defiant yowl, the sound piercing through the stillness of the forest. His fur bristled, and his tail puffed up as he continued to emit a series of cries, calling the Shadow to him. And the Shadow came. Like smoke taking shape, a swirling mass of blackness materialized from within the trees. Its form constantly shifted and changed as if it could not decide on a single shape. But its eyes were piercing and fixated on the cat.

Jax felt a shiver run down his spine but held his ground. He would not give it the pleasure of showing it his fear—not now. He had to lead the Shadow away and draw it deep into the forest's depths. With another defiant yowl, the black cat turned and darted past the Shadow into the woods. The Shadow pursued the feline, ready to destroy the animal.

Back at the Commune, Vonda had gathered twenty Circle members to form a protective circle in the center of the property. Analee and Sun-Moon started chanting the spell they had been practicing, their voices in combined harmony.

Once Relda and Armand returned, they would go to the forest to find the Shadow.

Meanwhile, at Armand's house, Relda and Armand scoured through the wreckage of his home. Who could have known about the knife? They must have known its significance. Was someone trying to stop them? Armand had no idea. They couldn't do anything more, so Relda suggested they return to the Commune.

Jax continued his daring game of cat and Shadow back in the forest, leading the entity deeper into the woods now shrouded in twilight. The dense trees seemed to close in on them. Jax could feel the Shadow's presence closing in and pressing against him, its desire to consume his soul again.

Jax was not alone as he ran from the Shadow. Starleenawas was with him. She told him the other trapped souls were scared but saw what was happening at the Commune, knowing a battle against the Shadow was coming. The trapped spirits were ready to assist in the fight, even if it meant punishment from the Shadow if it succeeded and killed them all.

With heavy hearts and weary steps, Relda and Armand trudged back to the trailer. The feeling of defeat weighed heavily on their shoulders as they delivered the news to Analee. The knife, which was needed for the spell, was gone.

Analee's voice trembled with desperation as she frantically asked, "How can we possibly move forward without it? The spell specifically calls for us to bring the Shadow into solid form and stab it with that knife."

Crox clenched his fists, his knuckles turning white. "We can't let this setback stop us," he said firmly. "We need to move forward. With or without this knife. There must be another way to Kill this thing."

Jax's daring game continued in the forest's depths. He and Starleena led the Shadow through a maze of trees and underbrush, keeping it at a distance while constantly taunting it. The entity's red eyes glowed fiercely with anger, its shape swirling and distorting in its pursuit of the cat.

Vonda came in to let the group know her protection circle was now complete. The Shadow should not be able to enter the Commune's property line. The Circle members would continue their protection spell until they returned after they sent the Shadow back to its realm or until morning if they did not live through the night. If he and the others failed, the group would abandon the Commune.

Crox, Analee, Armand, and Relda started to prepare for the confrontation. Without the enchanted silver knife, they needed to improvise. Analee and Sun-Moon were researching the spell book for an alternative way to hold back the Shadow before attempting the spell to make it solid. They knew they needed every advantage they could get.

Vonda continued to lead the Circle members, chanting their protection spell, their voices rising and falling in a bluesy rhythm. The air around the Commune crackled with electric energy, and a purple light barrier formed around the property.

"It's time to go." Armand stated. "Should we drive or walk?" asked Relda

Analee's voice trembled with desperation as she frantically asked, "How can we possibly move forward without it? The spell specifically calls for us to bring the Shadow into solid form and stab it with that knife."

"We will figure it out as we go; grab the spell book, and let's go," Crox answered.

The atmosphere seemed to shift as the group stepped out of the trailer to head to the circle of rocks deep in the forest, the place where the Shadow dwelled. The night air felt cool and moist. A sense of impending danger overtook him. He, along with Relda, Analee, Armand, Sun-Moon, and Vonda, made their way through the woods, guided by the faint light of the moon and the stars that now sparkled in the night sky.

Jax's diversion had led the Shadow deeper into the forest, away from the trapped souls and the Commune. The cat knew he could not keep this up forever; he was growing tired, and the Shadow's relentless pursuit was wearing him down. He had to keep the entity's attention focused on him until he and the others could confront it at the altar, where their power would be strongest.

The lost, trapped souls gathered at the sacred altar, the place in the woods with the circle of rocks where he had found Jax. They waited patiently to serve their purpose.

The forest seemed to close around the group as they walked silently. The tension in the air was thick, each step taking them closer to their possible death. Armand held the book tightly. Inside, it had the spell he hoped would finally free them from the Shadow. If it failed, they all surely would die.

They finally reached the sacred altar, a clearing surrounded by tall trees, bathed in a soft glow from the moonlight filtering through the tree branches. The altar was a circle made of old stones, and a large pentagram burned into the ground in the middle of it.

Analee's voice echoed with desperation, her words trembling with urgency as she frantically pleaded, "How can we possibly move forward without it? The spell specifically calls for us to summon the Shadow and trap it in solid form before plunging the enchanted knife into its heart."

As they took their positions, Analee took Armand's spell book, opened it before them, and began the spell to bring forth the Shadow. Relda stood back and watched, her hand resting on her gun holstered at her side.

The incantations flowed from Analee's lips, and she urged the others to follow her lead. The wind picked up, swirling the fallen leaves and creating an eerie rustling sound. The pentagram on the ground began to glow with a faint lime-green light.

The ground beneath them rumbled, and the trees around them seemed to howl. He began to see spirits all around them, encircling the group. He could see Starleena staring at him, her eyes filled with conviction, as if she were saying, "You got this."

Jax came running from the woods, jumping into the pentagram's center. In his mind, he heard Jax say, *"The Shadow is coming. Now is the time to destroy It and send it back from where it came."*

Jax's sudden appearance in the pentagram's center started everyone, causing Analee to drop the spellbook. Armand yelled for her to pick it up and not lose concentration. Soon, the group again began to chant the spell to bring forth the Shadow before them. As they continued to chant, the ground trembled more violently. The pentagram's lime-green light intensified, casting an eerie light on the group's faces and causing Jax's eyes to glow almost translucently.

Relda's grip on her gun tightened. Her heart pounded in her chest as she watched the scene unfold before her, and her nerves were on high alert.

From the depths of the woods emerged a swirling mass of darkness, the very essence of the shadow and all its evil.

The creature was drawn to the pentagram and the gathering of the souls. Like a moth to the flame, it came. Eyes the color of burning embers fixated on Jax, and then they turned to Crox.

The spirits surrounded the group of the living and began chanting the spell, their voices rising and falling in a rhythm that echoed the beat of the living heartbeat. The Shadow saw them and became incensed with fury. The Shadow's attention was now on the spirits, its energy growing stronger.

Jax locked his eyes on the Shadow. He knew he had to keep the entity's attention on him. He leaped forward, darting around the edges of the pentagram, staying just out of the Shadow's reach.

As the Shadow focused on Jax once again, the darkness that the Shadow was made of began to stretch—the inky blackness coming toward the trapped souls. The spirits stood firm, channeling their collective energy into the protective barrier surrounding the group, repelling the Shadow's advances.

As the living and the dead continued their chant, the spirits started to take human form. He recognized Starleena as her spirit form became more solid. Beside her was his cousin Danny, who looked at him and smiled proudly. Standing next to Sun-Moon was a spirit wearing old-fashioned clothes; he instantly knew somehow it was the witch Victoria. She was edging the others on to continue their chanting.

All the spirits were becoming more solid, their features becoming more apparent with each passing moment. Their presence lent the spell an extra layer of power, and the protection spell seemed to grow stronger. A chilling howl came out of the Shadow as it rushed towards the stone circle, ready to kill them all and collect their souls.

CHAPTER 20

FOREST CATS

The Shadow lunged forward at the Circle, ready to kill them all and claim their souls. The dead and the living continued their relentless chanting, their voices intertwining into a powerful symphony that resonated through the clearing. The spell pushed the Shadow's advance back; it released an angry howl.

While embraced by the protection of the spell, Jax transformed from being a black cat back into his human form from within the pentagram's center. Crox joined in the chorus, chanting the spell to make the Shadow turn into a solid form. Starleena, now more solid and than translucent, walked into the circle, taking hold of her father's hand.

Relda staggered backward, falling to the ground. She did not know how to comprehend what she was seeing. People started appearing around the circle out of nowhere.

Since Relda did not see them as spirits, this sight was frightening and unfolding before her eyes. For the first time, she wanted to turn and run for her own safety. Relda picked herself up, looking at the group of people appearing out of thin air. She found her inner strength and stood her ground.

The lime-green glow around the pentagram grew stronger as the spell's power took hold. Crox could feel the power surging through his body. Then, in his left ear, he heard Sean Palmer say, "You're doing great. Keep it up." Crox looked beside him to see Sean's spirit, his translucent form becoming solid, just as the other spirits were. Crox had not seen Sean's spirit come out of the orange cat.

"Sean, what happened to you?" Cox asked, shaken to see his dead lover's ghost.

"Last year I stole the sacrificial knife from Armand and came here to the forest alone to kill the Shadow. I stupidly thought I would be able to defeat the creature. It killed me the moment I stepped foot into its dwelling. The Shadow knew I was coming and lay in wait for me. You are now our only hope to be free of it."

Gathering his focus, Crox turned back toward the pentagram circle. The powerful energy coursing through him became almost overwhelming, but he pushed through, channeling it into the incantation. The chant intensified as the living and dead together poured their collective energy into the spell. Armand, Analee, Vonda, and Sun-Moon seemed paralyzed within the light surrounding the pentagram. Their eyes rolled into the back of their heads. All you could see were the whites of their eyes. They reminded him of zombies from old Vodoo movies.

Though still shaken and unsure of herself, Relda became transfixed by the mesmerizing display.

It had been a shock to see people appear out of thin air around the rock circle, but as she looked closer, she noticed something extraordinary. These were not just random people; some were her ancestors, standing shoulder to shoulder with the other materialized people. Relda realized many of her family members had been trapped by the Shadow.

A pitched shriek of anger came from the Shadow's direction as it lunged forward again. Breaking through the crowd of the solidified spirits, it knocked them down as it came closer to the rock circle.

Jax and Starleena increased their efforts, pouring every ounce of their strength into the chant. Jax's voice rang out loud, piercing through the air and blending with the voices of the living and the spirits alike. Starleena's grip on her father's hand tightened as the Shadow approached the rock circle.

Crox's heart raced as he saw the shadow approaching. Sweat trickled down his brow as he concentrated on maintaining the chant, his eyes fixed on the pentagram's center. The lime-green glow now pulsated with a rhythm that matched the beat of his heart. The ground beneath the pentagram trembled as the Shadow drew nearer to them. Its swirling darkness started becoming more solid at the edges.

The spirits, now solid, attempted to push against the Shadow's advance. Solidified hands reached out, grasping at its form, trying to slow down its advance. Unfortunately, the Shadow was still more mist than solid, and their efforts were in vain as their hands slipped through the Shadow's form.

Relda's heart pounded in her chest as she watched the intense struggle unfolding before her. Fear had grounded her, but she now regained her courage. She realized she should not just stand by; she had to do something. Relda stepped forward and joined the group around the circle.

Relda did not know the words of the chant, nor did she have any supernatural ability, but she knew she had a connection to this place through her ancestors, who were now standing beside her. She closed her eyes, took a deep breath, and started humming softly, a song her grandmother taught her as a child.

Relda's voice joined the others, adding an unexpected layer of harmony. The energy from the circle seemed to respond to her presence as if her intention to help resonated with the spell. The lime-green glow intensified, and the ground beneath them shook even more vigorously.

Crox felt a surge of hope as he saw Relda join the group. The combined efforts of the living, the dead, and now Relda created a tidal wave of power. He felt like a conduit, channeling this immense energy into the spell meant to trap the Shadow.

As the Shadow pushed its way closer to the center of the crowd of the dead, he felt a blinding pain in his temples, then a voice in his head that seemed to emanate from the depths of his consciousness.

"You are now the new guardian of the forest, the one who bridges the realms," the voice echoed in his mind. "You cannot defeat me; I am eternal; I do not die. Stop this now, and I will allow you to live and rule over the Circle of the Eternal Shadow. Take your mother's place as leader of the Witches Three."

Crox gritted his teeth, his body trembling as he fought to maintain his focus. The voice was unsettling, its words weaving doubt and fear into his thoughts. Remembering the Shadow's threat to the living and the spirit world, Crox pushed aside the voice's attempts to sway him. Drawing on his inner strength and the support of those around him, he channeled all his might into the chant.

Crox's voice wavered momentarily, but then it surged back with renewed vigor. The spell's words resonated with an intensity that seemed to shake the very fabric of reality.

The shadow advanced on him, entering the middle of the pentagram where Jaxson and Starleena stood. The creature tore at Starleena's throat. Jaxson was able to push her out of the circle away from the Shadow's grasp. Now, only Jaxson and the Shadow were held within the power of the circle. The light turned from lime green to muddy purple. Both seemed to be held in animation within the pentagram.

Jaxson's face contorted as he faced off against the Shadow. The creature's darkness billowed around him, but he stood his ground within the circle's confines. The chant continued, its volume and intensity building as if it were echoing from the very depths of the earth.

Crox was scared for Jaxson, but he would not let up now. Not only was Jaxson trapped within the spell embrace, but now they all were. The spell had bound not only the Shadow to the circle but also all of the spirits and the living. If he failed, they would all surely die.

The voice in his head persisted, its words growing more insidious and tempting: "You cannot win. I am inevitable. Embrace your destiny as guardian of the forest, as leader of my coven. I offer you power beyond your imagination."

"No, "Crox whispered through clenched teeth, his voice shaky but determined. "I won't let you control me or allow you to control this forest any longer."

The Shadow roared in anger, its dark form writhing within the circle, struggling against the spell that bound it.

Jaxson stood firm, his eyes locked onto the swirling darkness before him. With a surge of renewed strength, he pushed back against the Shadow. The two locked in a dance of death.

The Shadow's insults were filled with anger and spite. "Do you really believe you can resist me? You are nothing without me. Accept your true fate or suffer the same punishment as your bitch of a mother."

Amid the Shadow's verbal assault, a new voice emerged. It was the voice of Starleena, who had recovered from the Shadow's attack and reentered the circle. She stood beside him, taking his hand.

"You can't break us," Starleena declared. Our blood and the power of the witch Victoria bind us together as one. Your darkness can't extinguish that. Come forth, Victoria, we call upon you. This evil you brought forth out of the darkness, now you must send it back from which it came. My goddess Victoria, we implore you."

The muddy purple light pulsated. The battle between the Shadow and Jaxson raged on, and the Shadow's assaults on his mind continued.

From the outer layer of the circle, a figure emerged and stepped forth into the light—a lady with fiery red hair wearing a flowing white dress—a classic beauty with milky white skin and bright, soulful green eyes.

Victoria, the long-lost witch, brought forth this creature and died at its hands. Her eyes held a deep sadness as they settled on him. It was as if she had been waiting for this moment, trapped between worlds until the balance could be restored.

Victoria's voice was haunting as she addressed the Shadow. "You were born from desperation for power, a creation that should never have been. I call upon the power within me, the power of the witches of the circle, to banish you from this realm."

Crox felt a rush of heat in his belly and rose to his head. A burst of electric energy flowed through his hands. The witch Victoria began to sing in a language he did not recognize. Her voice rose above the chanting and the howls of the Shadow.

Starleena, still holding his hand, stepped into the pentagram's circle, bringing him with her. He tried to pull back, but Starleena's grip tightened as she gently pulled him along. Her knowing smile put him at ease; she knew what must be done.

"Father, now it is time. Let the Shadow go into you. Welcome it into your body," Starleena said as she and Crox entered the purple light emanating from the circle's center.

Jaxson stopped fighting the Shadow and embraced it as if they were lovers. Suddenly, the Shadow turned into mist, entering through his mouth, nose, and eyes. As this was happening, Starleena looked at him and said,

"Take the blade from your boot and stab your brother through the heart."

Crox's eyes widened in shock at Starleena's words. "What? I can't stab my brother."

"You must. It is the only way to rid the Shadow from this realm. Please, Uncle, this is the only way to save us from the Shadow's grasp."

He trembled. He glanced at the blade in his boot and then back at Jaxson, who was now entwined with the Shadow. The entity seemed to have merged with him, and he could see the torment in Jaxson's eyes as he struggled to maintain control of his mind.

Taking a deep breath, he slowly withdrew the blade from his boot. His heart pounded in his chest, and his hands shook as he held the weapon. The chanting around him intensified. Jaxson yelled out, "Now, brother, stab me, send it back from where it came."

With tears in his eyes, Crox steeled himself and lunged forward, thrusting the blade into Jaxson's heart. Jaxson's eyes widened in shock and pain, his mental grip on the Shadow faltering momentarily. As the knife pierced his chest, an anguished cry tore from Jaxson's lips. The electric energy around them surged, the light turning blindingly bright before dimming down. A chilling wail that seemed to echo across dimensions seemed to come from every direction of the forest.

As Jaxson fell to the ground, he saw the most fantastic thing. Jaxson reverted to his feline form and the Shadow turned to mist, slowly vanishing into nothingness. All around him, Crox saw the solidness of the spirits beginning to shrink and transform; in a matter of seconds, hundreds of cats surrounded him. All of the spirits turned into cats.

The spell seemed broken, releasing Sun-Moon, Armand, Analee, and Vonda. They stood there, dumbfounded, looking down at all the cats. Relda walked up to him and asked, "Are you okay? Is it over?" Then she said, "What's with all these cats?"

Crox took a deep breath, his body trembling from the emotional and physical strain he had just endured. Crox looked around at the scene before him, the forest filled with cats of all colors and sizes.

"I think...I think it's over," Crox managed to say in a weak voice. He looked at Relda and smiled at her. "I believe a part of the Shadow was a part of Jax, or should I say Jaxson. Stapping him with the enchanted knife separated them and I believe the Shadow is now gone, back to its realm. It no longer has an anchor to our world. As for the cats, I think they're the spirits of all of the souls that the Shadow had trapped. Somehow, the spell transformed them into this form."

Relda's eyes widened. "Incredible," she whispered. I Have never seen anything like this. But what about Jaxson? Is he...?"

Crox looked down at the unconscious cat, Jaxson had transformed back into his cat form. He knelt beside the feline, carefully picking him up and cradling him in his arms. Jax's breathing was shallow, and he could feel his heart racing. "He's alive. Let's get him out of here."

The group walked back to the Commune wearily, leaving behind hundreds of cats to roam the forest.

Analee was the first to speak. "Thank you. We are free from the Shadow; there is no longer a need for the Circle of the Eternal Shadow."

When they reached the trailer, the cult members who had stayed behind to provide the protection spell to protect the commune ran to them, happy to see they were still alive. After Vonda filled them in, she directed them to leave and not return; the circle was broken. This was no longer a place for them. Crox would decide what to do with the property.

Armand andAnalee left next. He had told Armand he had been rehired and expected him to return to work. Analee told him she would be there for him if he needed anything.

Before Vonda and Sun-Moon left, Crox thanked them for their help and told Vonda he understood what she had tried to do. There were no hard feelings; all was forgiven.

Left alone, Relda and Crox stepped outside, letting Jax sleep quietly on the couch. Staring up at the bright moon, he looked at Relda and said, "I guess now the cats are the new guardians of the forest."

"Yes," Relds said slowly, her eyes darting to the dark woods. "But what else could be lurking in those foreboding trees?" Her words were tinged with caution and unease as if she already knew the answer but was afraid to say it out loud.

The sky was a painting of churning, ominous clouds that loomed low over the thick forest, casting it in a shroud of darkness. The trees below were cloaked in deep shadows as if concealing secrets within their gnarled branches.

In the distance, the eerie howling of wolves reverberated through the eerie stillness of the air, causing Crox and Jax to shudder. Their cries were chilling and seemed like a warning of unknown dangers lurking in the depths of the woods. What other horrors awaited them?

This would not be the end of their supernatural fight against evil.

Made in United States
Troutdale, OR
03/28/2025